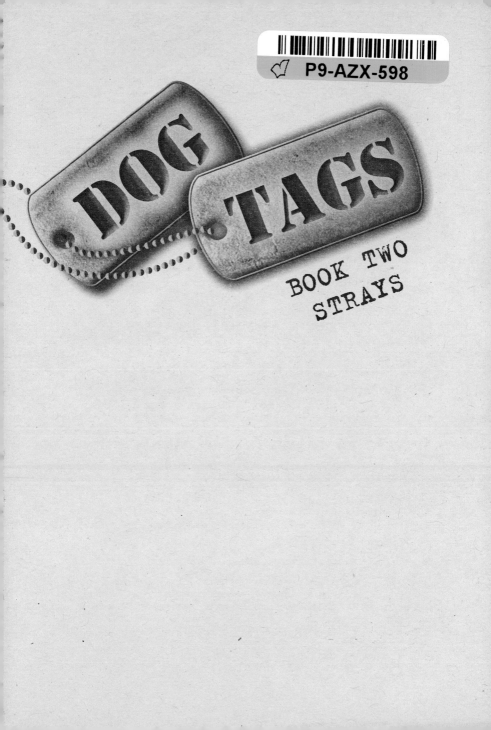

DOG TAGS

BOOK TWO
STRAYS

DOG TAGS

BOOK TWO
STRAYS

C. ALEXANDER LONDON

SCHOLASTIC INC.

No part of this publication may be reproduced, stored in a retrieval system, or transmitted in any form or by any means, electronic, mechanical, photocopying, recording, or otherwise, without written permission of the publisher. For information regarding permission, write to Scholastic Inc., Attention: Permissions Department, 557 Broadway, New York, NY 10012.

ISBN 978-0-545-47705-5

Copyright © 2012 by C. Alexander London
All rights reserved. Published by Scholastic Inc.
SCHOLASTIC and associated logos are trademarks and/or registered trademarks of Scholastic Inc.

10 9 8 7 6 5 4 3 2 1   12 13 14 15 16

Printed in the U.S.A.   40
First printing, September 2012

To the dogs, in memoriam.

Listen to the moan of a dog for its master.

That whining is the connection.

There are love dogs no one knows the names of.

Give your life to be one of them.

— Jalaluddin Rumi, translated by Coleman Barks

CHAPTER 1

GOOD TIMES

It was a good time. Double O was beaten and Billy Beans had lost and Doc Malloy went down in a shutout, twenty-one to nothing. They were all among the losers. Chuck Perkins was unbeatable.

They called him the King of Ping, the master of the paddle. He sat beneath the shade of a rubber tree beside the ping-pong table, reading a dog-eared paperback of *Don Quixote* that someone had left behind, and waited for a new challenger. The book was old, but it wasn't bad, all about a crazy man who had read too many books and convinced himself that he was a knight.

While he waited, Chuck scratched Ajax behind the ears with his free hand.

"Good boy," he murmured to his dog. Ajax was a great big German shepherd with a shiny coat of black-and-brown fur, flecks of white on his snout, and a giant pink tongue hanging out to the left, panting in the sticky afternoon heat. "I wish you could play ping-pong. Maybe you'd be a real challenger. Not like these bozos."

He looked around. No one was watching him talk to his dog. Ajax looked up at him with his patient brown eyes, much more at peace with lying around than Chuck was.

"No takers?" Chuck called out, stretching the boredom out of his limbs. "Don't be scared! I'll let you serve the whole time!"

Ajax cocked his head at his master.

"What?" said Chuck. "I'll still win."

Ajax scratched his neck with his back paw and settled down onto the ground to snooze the afternoon away in the shade. It was too hot to do much else. They hadn't had a mission to go out on in a week, hadn't had contact with the enemy in longer than that, and all the soldiers at the remote jungle outpost were bored. Chuck, at least, had Ajax to keep him entertained. Well, he had Ajax and the old book, and he had ping-pong.

It was a good time, thought Chuck.

As far as the war in Vietnam went, it was a pretty good time for sure.

Chuck went back to his book, still idly petting his dog. Growing up, he had always wanted a dog, but his parents never let him get one. They said he wasn't responsible enough.

Well, look at me now, he thought to himself. He was the best army scout-dog handler in Vietnam, responsible for protecting every patrol he went out on from ambushes and booby traps, and responsible for the care of his dog in harsh jungle conditions. In the letters he sent home to his mom and dad, he made sure to rub it in.

He thought about writing them another letter. They missed him terribly and hoped he'd come home soon. But he didn't feel like writing right now. He felt like playing ping-pong, and he wished someone would come over for a game.

The rule on the small base was that whoever won the last game of ping-pong had dibs on the table. Was it his fault that he was better at it than everyone else?

Chuck believed in the rules.

He believed in the big rules of the United States military — like following orders and saluting the officers — and he believed in the little rules, the unspoken rules among the men that were known by everybody without ever being told to anybody.

Like dibs.

You couldn't start just ignoring some rules because you didn't like them. The rules kept society together. Without the rules, the men of the infantry brigades sprinkled across the hills and jungles of Vietnam would be just a bunch of teenagers with guns wandering around a foreign country. The rules made them an army.

Chuck sighed and went back to his book. The brave knight had spurred his horse on to attack some windmills, which he thought were giants. The scene would have been funny, if it weren't so hard to get through. Chuck wasn't the best reader in the world, and the book wasn't the easiest. But no one came over to challenge him to a game, so he passed the afternoon reading *Don Quixote* and petting his dog. He couldn't imagine what else the others were up to that was more fun than ping-pong.

Across the small infantry outpost, on the other side of the plywood headquarters building, Double O, Billy Beans, and Doc Malloy were crouched behind some sandbags, discussing their ping-pong problem.

"Chuck's got to go down," Double O declared. "He been holding that table all week. What if the brothers want to get a game?"

"The brothers can just wait their turn," sneered Billy Beans, who never had a nice word for Double O.

"If we wait for some farm boy to win a game, we be waiting until the war in Vietnam's over," said Double O, laughing. He enjoyed doing what he could to annoy Billy Beans.

Billy wasn't one of those real racists, like the drill sergeant back in Georgia who had called Double O every name in the book (and some that hadn't been written down yet). He was just a country boy from Nowheresville who had never known a black person before he was drafted to fight the war in Vietnam.

But he was a good soldier — hardworking and loyal — and that's all that mattered out in the bush. Even if Double O didn't like him, he trusted Billy Beans when it counted. Also, when Billy got mad, his face turned red as strawberry soda, and Double O loved to make that happen. It passed the time.

"What we gotta do," said Double O, "is get Chuck away from that table long enough to take it back from him. Chuck's short for Charlie, right?"

"You don't know that?" Billy Beans was often shocked by what Double O didn't know. Like when they were out on patrol near that village and they saw a girl milking a water buffalo. Double O just stood and stared at her, his rifle slack at his side.

"She's just milking her buffalo," Billy had said. "You never see an animal get milked before?"

"Only milk I ever drank came from a case in the back of the corner store," Double O said. "Not from some hairy giant in the jungle."

Billy Beans could only shake his head. He'd been milking cows since he could walk; a water buffalo wasn't so different. He'd never understand city boys.

"My point is," Double O said now, "Chuck is short for Charlie . . . so we treat Chuck like we treat Charlie. Seize the table like it's a VC weapons stash."

VC stood for Vietcong. Victor-Charlie, sometimes just Charlie. They had so many names for the same thing: the enemy.

It was Chuck's bad luck to share the name.

Stuck on base for over a week with no missions to go out on, no attacks from the Vietcong to repel, the guys were starting to go a little nuts.

The news back home showed all kinds of pictures of violence from the war in Vietnam: wounded soldiers and dead Vietnamese stacked like cordwood, bombs raining down on the jungle. In American cities, protesters marched against the war. Some even called the returning soldiers "baby killers" and spat on them in the streets. To hear the news, you'd think that the war was nothing but death and destruction and discord, but the news never said anything about how dull war could be.

There were rumors that it was almost over. Peace talks were happening in Paris. Old men in suits sat around big tables deciding the fate of all the young men with guns. The president had promised to bring the soldiers home.

Billy wondered if he'd already missed the war. How could he show his face to his high school buddies back home if he hadn't been in combat — real combat? All he'd done so far was slog through the jungle, wade through the muck of rice paddies, and search village after village, patting down women, children, and old men. He never saw any young men in the villages. Just the very old and the very young and the very weak and the very tired.

He still hadn't seen the enemy. He'd never even fired his gun. The only time they ever got attacked, he was in the middle of the line and all he could do was hit the ground and wait for it to be over, which it was, in minutes. There was shooting and then there wasn't, and the enemy had vanished again. He couldn't get a good war story out of that. If the war ended before he got the chance to shoot at something, he'd never be able to convince Nancy Werner to go out with him. He needed to do something brave.

It wasn't combat and it wasn't brave, but a mission to seize the ping-pong table would at least be *something* to do for now, except that Double O had failed to consider one very important detail.

"We cannot sneak up on Chuck," Billy explained in case Double O didn't know about dogs the same way he didn't know about water buffalo. "He's always got Ajax with him, and that dog goes after anyone who even looks at Chuck funny. Did you see when Sergeant Cody came by to yell at Chuck for his hair being too long? Ajax almost ripped off the man's blond head, sent him scrambling out of the tent on his backside. I'm not about to tangle with Chuck while Ajax is around."

"No tangling, Billy." Double O smiled. He slapped at a mosquito on his arm, leaving a mushy red splotch where it bit him. "You talkin' to Double O, after all. I'm the James

Bond of Brooklyn." He turned to look at the platoon's medic, Robert "Doc" Malloy. "And I've got a plan."

"I don't like that devious look of yours," said Doc, holding up his hands, palms out, like he was trying to push Double O's plan away.

"You just gonna give the dog a once-over is all," said Double O. "Urgent medical something or other."

"I'm not a veterinarian," said Doc.

"You're not a doctor either," Double O replied. "You just the guy with the bandages and a few weeks of training."

"Still, it's not right to use my training to ambush a ping-pong table."

"You ain't ambushing nothing," Double O explained. "You just got to get the dog tied up to check him for . . . what? Like, fleas or something. And once he's tied up, we rush the table."

"And then me and you do what?" Billy asked. "Tie *Chuck* up?"

"You and I," corrected Double O. "And yes, what you and I do is we tie Chuck up. If he don't surrender quietly."

The three men crouched silently, thinking over their plan, looking for flaws, considering their options. It felt good having a mission to think about.

"So once we get the table back, who gets the first game?" Billy broke the silence.

"We play for it," said Double O. "I win, it's the brothers' table. You win, you do what you want."

"And what about me?" said Doc. "Where do I fit in?"

"With Billy, I suppose."

"Oh, don't do that. Just 'cause we're white, huh?"

"No, Doc, just 'cause you terrible at ping-pong. You try to play with us, you gonna lose even worse than you lost to Chuck."

"What's worse than losing twenty-one to nothing?" Doc wondered. "You can't do worse than nothing. Nothing is nothing."

Double O just shrugged. It was a deep question — "What was worse than nothing?" — and the day was too hot and too sticky to think about deep questions. If he were back in Brooklyn, it would have been a stoop day, a day to just sit outside on the stoop and watch the girls walk past, a day to maybe open up a fire hydrant to cool off.

But in Vietnam, there wasn't any way to cool off, not for the combat infantry grunts of the United States Army. If they weren't hiking through the stinking jungle on some long patrol, wearing through their boots and their feet, they were sitting bored on some base, sweating through the days and nights until they had to go out into the bush again.

He wasn't even sure why they were fighting a war in Vietnam. Nobody was. Something about stopping the spread of communism in Southeast Asia, protecting the free world for democracy and all that. The *why*s of war didn't matter so much when you were the guy on the ground fighting it. Double O cared more about the *when*s of war, like "When do we eat?", and "When do we fight?", and most of all, "When do we get to go home?"

But he couldn't answer those questions either.

"So, you good ol' boys in or what?" Double O wiped his hands on his pants and stood. "Because I want to get a game in before chow time."

"I'm in." Doc Malloy sighed. He didn't like to abuse his position as the platoon medic, but he also didn't like being embarrassed at the ping-pong table.

And anyway, until they got a real combat mission, the Siege of the Pong against Ajax the scout dog and his handler, Chuck, would pass the time.

In this war, passing the time was the best anyone could do.

CHAPTER 2

THE SIEGE OF THE PONG

Chuck stopped reading when Ajax let out a low growl. His ears pointed straight up. Chuck could see the four-digit serial number that the army had tattooed on the soft pink flesh inside the scout dog's ear.

Chuck had learned to understand the movement of Ajax's ears and the tone of his growls the way best friends understand each other's shrugs and sighs. After all this time together, there wasn't much Ajax could do that Chuck didn't understand. And right now, Ajax was giving Chuck a warning.

"What is it, Doc?" Chuck said, without looking up.

"I, uh . . . I . . ." Doc Malloy stumbled, spooked that Chuck knew he was there without even looking up.

Chuck liked the rest of the platoon to think he and Ajax possessed some kind of mystical power, when really, it was

12

just that he spent more time with his dog than he did with most humans. He rotated in and out of different army units every few weeks, so he never had time to make friends. The only constant companion he had was Ajax.

Also, it helped that Doc cast an unmistakable shadow. In spite of all the marching and the terrible military food, Doc was round.

"Relax, Doc," said Chuck. "Ajax won't attack . . . unless I tell him to."

Doc nodded, standing on the opposite side of the ping-pong table, frozen in place. Despite Chuck's assurance, he obviously thought that any sudden movement might alarm the big German shepherd.

He was probably right, but Ajax had learned the smell of every soldier in the platoon and he knew who was friendly and who wasn't.

Of course, even friends could turn on you.

In the scout-dog handler course Chuck had taken at Fort Benning, Georgia, one of the first lessons they'd learned was to treat their dogs with respect. Dogs were man's best friends, but they were still animals, and Ajax had enough power in his jaws to tear a man's arm off. When they'd first met, Chuck had been a little frightened of the muscular German shepherd. Now, he couldn't imagine a better dog in all the world.

"So, you come for another game?" Chuck set his book down and stood. He was happy for something else to do. The book was good, but kind of hard to understand. There were a lot of *thee*s and *thou*s and long speeches about romance and honor and heroism. It was very old-fashioned. "I'm glad you're not embarrassed to try again. No shame in losing to the best, right? Maybe you'll even score a point this time. Your serve."

He tossed Doc the ping-pong ball.

"I'm not here to, uh, play," said Doc, setting the ball carefully on the table beneath the paddle. "I . . ."

"You look nervous."

"Dogs make me nervous."

"You know, Ajax can smell fear," Chuck explained. "If he smells that you're afraid, he'll start to think maybe there's something around here to be afraid of . . . and we don't want him getting jumpy, do we?"

"No, we don't," said Doc. "See, I've got to check him, for . . . you know, uh . . . fleas?"

"Is that a question?"

"What?"

"Were you telling me or asking me?"

"Telling you. I've got to check Ajax for fleas."

"You aren't a veterinarian."

"That's what I told them."

"Told who?"

"What?"

"Who did you tell you weren't a veterinarian?"

"Uh . . ."

Chuck didn't need Ajax's highly developed senses to know something was wrong. Doc was acting weird. He'd been on patrol with Ajax a half-dozen times without ever getting weird around the dog. So if it wasn't the dog making him nervous, then it was something new. And "something new" made Chuck suspicious.

He narrowed his eyes at Doc Malloy. "Fleas, huh?"

"Yeah, fleas. Gotta tie Ajax up to check him. You know, for safety."

"Yeah," said Chuck, looking at Doc. "Safety."

They stared at each other across the ping-pong table. Doc stood as still as a statue, trying to keep his face from betraying him, and Chuck let a slight smirk pull at the corners of his mouth. At Chuck's side, Ajax had his ears up and was watching Doc Malloy closely.

15

"What's going on?" whispered Billy Beans. He had ducked behind a pile of sandbags and pressed his back against it, like he was taking cover from enemy fire.

"Doc's giving up the game," said Double O, peering over the top of the sandbags. "That dog can smell his fear. Shoot, I can smell it from over here."

"What do we do?" said Billy. "We can't get the table unless Ajax is tied up."

"I know that," said Double O. "Let me think."

"I knew this was a bad idea," said Billy. "I knew he wouldn't fall for it. I mean, the man's on his fourth tour of duty in Vietnam. He *volunteered* to come back, you know. Who does that? Who would choose to come back to the war in Vietnam when it ain't his turn? He's crazy. You can't mess with someone who's crazy."

"Calm down, Billy." Double O shook his head. "Chuck may be crazy, but he doesn't read minds. If Doc keeps his cool, we'll be in the clear."

Double O looked back at the ping-pong table, where Doc was *not* keeping his cool. He was talking fast and flapping his hands in the air like a bird, and then he looked over at the sandbags and pointed, and Chuck looked their way.

"Shoot." Double O ducked down next to Billy, pressing himself against the sandbags. His heart beat against his rib cage. He held his breath.

"Did he see us?" Billy asked, chewing his lower lip. "Did he see? What's happening?"

"Quiet," Double O snapped, waiting. He listened to the breeze passing through the trees around the base. Somewhere in the distance, a monkey screeched. Double O had to ask himself what the heck he was up to. He should be at home in Brooklyn, not over here in Vietnam fighting someone else's war. Shoot, he wasn't even fighting. He was hiding behind some sandbags so that he could get control of a ping-pong table on a tiny base in the middle of the jungle. He shook his head and pushed himself off the ground.

"What are you doing?" Billy whispered, frantic.

"This is stupid," said Double O.

"But it was your idea!"

Double O stood up, ready to swallow his pride and ask Chuck for a rematch, fair and square. But instead, he found himself staring right into the slobbering jaws of Ajax. A few feet behind the dog, Chuck smiled widely.

"You surrender?" said Chuck, laughing.

"I'm sorry!" Doc Malloy called from behind Chuck. "He traded me two cans of peaches to give you up!"

"Traitor!" Billy Beans called without standing up, although he knew that he too would have betrayed them for two extra cans of peaches. They were the only decent rations the army gave out and they were worth more on this little base than anything.

Double O didn't make a sound. He didn't dare even move. Ajax rumbled, a low-belly growl.

"I'd stay still if I were you," Chuck told Double O.

"I ain't moving," Double O whispered. He remembered the junkyard dog by his grandmother's house that had terrorized him and his cousins whenever they'd lost a ball over the fence.

"You gotta admit," said Chuck. "You didn't even hear Ajax coming."

"I admit. He a heck of a dog. Just call him off, Chuck."

"Ajax!" Chuck called. Ajax's ears perked up. All his muscles tensed. Double O closed his eyes. "Kiss!" said Chuck, and Double O felt a big wet tongue crash into his face and douse him with doggy drool.

"Gah!" He fell backward and Ajax jumped right on top

of him, licking his face like a popsicle. "This ain't right, Chuck! Get him off me!"

Billy Beans and Doc Malloy were laughing like madmen.

"I taught him that a few days ago," said Chuck. "Been dying to see if he'd do it."

Double O pushed and struggled, but the German shepherd would not let him out from underneath his paws. Ajax had him pinned, and Double O was soaked with drool when Chuck finally called the dog off. Then Chuck helped Double O to his feet.

"You crazy, you know that?" said Double O.

"I've heard it before." Chuck smiled.

Double O shook his head and spat on the ground. Ajax knocked at his hand with his nose, demanding to be petted.

"I think Ajax might be in love with you," laughed Billy Beans.

"Oh, shut your mouth, Beans," Double O snapped at him. He knew it was all in fun — he'd been ready to tie Chuck up a few minutes ago — but his pride was hurt and he wasn't about to be mocked by Billy Beans. What kind of a name was *Beans*, anyway? If he let Billy Beans get away with making fun of him now, he'd get away with making fun of him forever.

"You kiss so good," Billy cackled.

"I said shut it!" Double O yelled and gave Billy a shove. Billy tripped over his own heel and went sprawling backward into the mud.

Like a jack-in-the-box, Billy popped up again, all the heat and boredom of the days with nothing to do boiling over in a red-faced rage. He clenched his fist and took a swing at Double O, who ducked out of the way and elbowed him in the side. Ajax barked, but Chuck caught him by the collar and held him tight as Billy scrambled around to take another swing at Double O: a wide right that missed. Double O caught him with another quick jab in the ribs. Billy elbowed him in the jaw and tried to get him in a headlock.

"What is wrong with you?" Billy grunted. "You crazy —"

"Cut it out right now!" A yell tore through their fight. They let go of each other and stood rigid at attention. Doc Malloy and Chuck also snapped to attention, with Ajax sitting alert at Chuck's feet. Lieutenant Maxwell, the platoon commander and the most senior officer on the base, came rushing over. "What's the problem here, Doc?" He addressed Doc Malloy, who was the oldest of the group.

"Just a friendly misunderstanding, sir," said Doc, following another of those unspoken rules. You don't rat out other enlisted men to an officer.

"That right?" said the lieutenant, looking Billy and Double O up and down.

"Yes, sir!" Double O and Billy said in unison, staring forward.

"I know it's dull as dirt out here," said the lieutenant. "But I need you guys to keep your cool. You're my fifth fight today. We'll get a mission soon, I promise."

"Yes, sir," they said again.

The lieutenant nodded and walked away, muttering to himself. He probably never thought when he became an officer in the United States Army that he'd have to break up fights between his own men like a teacher on a playground. He was only twenty-two years old, after all — barely old enough to be a teacher, let alone a leader of men at war. But so it goes.

After he was gone, Double O turned to Billy. "You stay the hell away from me," he said, and walked past him, knocking him hard with his shoulder.

"What's his problem?" Billy muttered.

Chuck picked up the ping-pong paddles, clipped Ajax to his leash, and walked off to practice Ajax's commands. If they did get a mission into the jungle, Chuck wanted them to be at their best. All this drama between people didn't really interest him.

Chuck wished people could be more like Ajax. Ajax didn't care about the color of your skin or if you made fun of him or called him names. Ajax didn't hold a grudge. Ajax just liked to play. Chuck liked to play too. Why'd everything have to get so serious all the time? Didn't these guys know that life was too short for that kind of nonsense?

Maybe they didn't.

They hadn't seen fighting like Chuck had. This was his fourth tour of duty in Vietnam, after all. The guys were on their first, probably their only. They hadn't been in the bush as deep or as long as Chuck. They hadn't watched friends die, blown to bits by land mines, shot to pieces by enemy guns, skewered like roast pigs on the end of sharpened bamboo sticks buried in the dirt.

They hadn't walked point — that position at the front of a patrol — and known with every step that the enemy could

22

be watching, ready, waiting to cut their lives off before they'd really even begun.

Chuck had.

Chuck knew.

Chuck had seen it all and done it all, and he'd keep doing it until the war was over.

The mission came.

Second platoon was ordered to fly into the valley to the north and cut across the jungle toward the river, clearing out the enemy as they went. They were told to pack enough food and water for three days. For Chuck, that meant enough for himself and for Ajax.

He started packing the supplies into his backpack as neatly as he could so he could get what he needed quickly. Ajax was curled up just outside their tent, tied to a stake in the ground. When Sergeant Cody came in to tell them to pack as much ammunition as they could carry, Chuck smiled the whole time. The sergeant, whose bright blond hair made Chuck think of the Beach Boys, had been afraid of Ajax since they met. Ajax let out a low growl until the sergeant left.

"What's the point of all this?" Double O wondered, taking a few ration cans out of his bag — beef and beans, spaghetti with meatballs, sliced peaches, and enough Tabasco sauce to burn down the whole jungle — and rearranging them to make more room for bullets. "They ain't heard the news? The war's about over. Why we gotta go hunt for VC when we outta here soon?"

Chuck kept working on his own backpack. He didn't turn around, but he listened closely, wondering if what Double O said was true. Hoping.

"How do you know the war's ending?" Doc Malloy asked him.

"Friend back in New York wrote me a letter," said Double O. "Peace talks in Paris, France."

"Why they do the peace talks in France?" Billy wondered.

Double O ignored him.

"Vietnam used to be a French colony," Doc Malloy explained. "The Vietnamese fought the French out, and then the communists came in. When the communists came in, the United States came in to fight *them* out. Now Double

O says we're being shown the exit door, although I think the communists still have some fight in them."

Billy nodded like he understood, but he didn't understand. Politics didn't really matter to him and he didn't try to learn much about them. He just wanted to see some action and get back to Minnesota to tell the tale to Nancy Werner. Maybe get a medal on his chest before he left. But if Double O was right, if the war was about over, this mission might be his last chance.

"See, Doc," said Double O, "I got no quarrel with the communists. This is a problem between the Vietnamese themselves. Let them sort it out. I got no reason to kill Vietnamese folks. It's not my war. My war's back home in places like Selma, Alabama, and Memphis, Tennessee. No Vietnamese ever made me sit at the back of no bus."

"Could you knock it off with the politics?" Billy cut him off. "None of that stuff matters. We're here, we fight like we're told."

"Shoot, these mosquitoes be buzzing loud today," Double O said, without turning to look at Billy Beans.

Billy looked at Doc for some help.

"Billy's got a point, you know," Doc said. "We're here. We fight until they tell us to stop. That's the job."

26

"Hey, man, I didn't sign up to be here. I was drafted."

"We were *all* drafted," said Billy. "But you don't hear us griping about it every five minutes."

"Chuck wasn't drafted," said Doc. "Chuck volunteered."

"I was drafted the first time," Chuck corrected him.

"Now, I can't for the life of me imagine why anyone would get drafted, do their time for Uncle Sam, and then come back and do it again four times," said Double O.

Chuck stopped packing his rucksack and turned to face Doc and Billy and Double O.

"Ajax," he said. "I got Ajax in '68 and I reenlisted to stay with him." He went back to shoving gear into his bag. "I just hope you're right about the war ending. Because if this isn't your war, it's not my war either, and it sure isn't Ajax's war. He was drafted just like the rest of you."

"Well, we're all in it now," said Doc, turning to Double O. "And before it's over, we're going into the bush, and I'd like us all to come back in one piece. That means we've got to stay focused, and whatever you and Billy have going on needs to be left in the past. Forget history. Put it behind you. You ready to do that?"

"I am," said Billy eagerly.

"In the past, huh?" Double O looked Billy up and down.

Billy tensed, clenching his jaw as if expecting to take a punch. Double O sighed. "Shoot, seems like it's always brothers bein' told to forget history. Guess I'm a pro at it by now."

He put his hand out and gave Billy a fist bump.

"We good?" said Billy.

Double O shrugged. "Good enough."

"Good," said Doc. "No more griping from either of you. It's time to shoot straight."

"I can gripe *and* shoot straight," said Double O. "Two things I learned best in basic training: guns and complaining."

Doc chuckled.

"Yeah," Double O laughed. "Sounds like one of Billy's redneck songs."

"Uncle Sam don't care if you're complain-ing, long as you shoot straight in basic train-ing!" sang Billy with an exaggerated twang, tapping his foot and moving his arm back and forth like he was playing a fiddle. The guys all laughed.

As the hour got closer, the men of second platoon got quieter. A few wrote emotional letters home. Others just stared off into the jungle, trying to read it like a fortune-teller reads a crystal ball. Although, if the jungle had secrets to tell about the future, it wasn't telling it to them.

Chuck walked with Ajax to the ping-pong table and pulled his utility knife from his belt. The dog panted up at him, his ears pointed to the sky and his nose twitching at the air.

"You ready to go out again, pal?" Chuck asked.

Chuck led him to the tree next to the table, where Ajax lifted his leg and peed.

"That's right, Ajax," said Chuck. "Mark your spot. We were here."

Chuck spent the next fifteen minutes making his own mark, carving it deep into the weeping trunk of the rubber tree:

Chuck P + Ajax were here. Devil Dogs. Undefeated.

He stood back and looked at his work, with Ajax sitting at his heels. He rested his hand on his dog's head and closed his eyes, breathing in the last moments of quiet before he heard the slap of the helicopter blades approaching to take him and his partner back into the war.

CHAPTER 4

A LONG AND LONELY WALK

The helicopters had gone and left them and now the only sounds were jungle sounds. The platoon stretched out single-file. Chuck let Ajax sniff at every guy in line to memorize their scents as they went past. Once they stepped out into the jungle, if Ajax picked up the scent of a new person, he'd know it wasn't one of theirs. Some of the guys shifted nervously as Ajax sniffed them.

"Don't you dare let that dog bite me," Sergeant Cody grumbled. A few of the privates smirked when Ajax nuzzled into their crotches. A few winced. But everyone nodded gratefully at Chuck. No one liked to walk point. It was the most dangerous position, the first in line, and they were all glad it'd be him instead of them.

Chuck and Ajax got to the front. Double O and his big sixty-caliber machine gun were next in line, and some private whose name Chuck didn't know was with Double O, hauling the heavy cans of ammo for the belt-fed machine gun. Double O had two bandoliers of bullets over his shoulders. They looped across his chest in an X like on a bad guy in an old Western.

Chuck looked down the line behind him once more. A column of black and white faces looked back, all of them young faces, all of them grim and thoughtful. Every man was a little lost in his thoughts, clutching his gun. Some of them tapped their fingers nervously on the stocks of their M16s. Some of them shifted their weight from foot to foot. Some were still as statues, waiting for the long slog into the jungle. Chuck had been in Vietnam long enough to know it was likely that not all of them would be walking out again.

Billy Beans and Doc Malloy were in the second squad back, about fifteen people behind Chuck. The lieutenant and his radioman were back with Billy, and the sergeant was all the way in the rear, keeping his eye on the line to make sure nobody fell behind or talked loud or messed up in any way that put their mission or their lives in danger. Chuck figured it was also the sergeant's way of staying as far as he could from Ajax. There was no love lost between the sergeant and Chuck's scout dog. But if they each did their jobs, maybe they would all walk out of the jungle again, each and every one of them.

The whole scene made Chuck think about elementary school, when all the kids would line up in the classroom, waiting to go to recess. There was fidgeting and nervous anticipation and excitement about games of dodgeball or Red Rover, the boys all wondering who would get to pick teams, who would get picked first, who would get picked last.

Thinking about when he was a schoolkid made Chuck's mouth go chalky and his eyes tear up. He shook the thoughts from his head, like Ajax shaking water from his fur. Chuck knew that if he let memories in, let fears in, let anything in but the job ahead of him, he'd never have the nerve to do what needed to be done.

He had to walk point through the jungle.

Walking point meant the front of the line, on his own, only Ajax for company, only Ajax's senses to warn him of an ambush or a booby trap. The jungle was littered with traps, and all of them were designed to kill American soldiers.

There were trip wires attached to land mines and hand grenades — tiny strands, almost invisible. The enemy hid them in the thick brush of the jungle. One wrong step and *BOOM!*

Then there were the punji stakes. The VC took bamboo sticks and sharpened them into points. They'd bury them in the dirt at an angle and cover them with leaves so that a man wouldn't see them until he'd impaled himself. Sometimes they buried them in pits and covered the pits with a thin layer of dirt and brush. An unsuspecting soldier would fall right through and get skewered like a suckling pig at a barbecue. They'd often smear the sticks with chili peppers to make the wounds hurt more . . . or with human waste to make sure the wounds got infected.

It was disgusting, but effective. The greatest army in the world was being stopped in its tracks by spicy, poop-covered sticks.

Of course, the VC would try anything to stop the Americans. They were fighting for their own country, after all. Most of the American soldiers didn't even know what they were fighting for. At least Chuck knew. He was fighting for Ajax.

The lieutenant signaled for the column to move out.

"Okay, Ajax," Chuck told his dog. "Let's get to work."

As they zigzagged to the tree line, Chuck waded through elephant grass as high as his waist. Ajax vanished beneath it, his leash rising up to Chuck's hands from a sea of green. It was impossible to see the ground. Survival was a matter of faith now, of trusting his dog to alert him to threats before they could hurt him.

They slipped from the tall grass beneath towering jungle trees and entered the shady confines of the jungle single-file.

Chuck followed wherever Ajax went. If Ajax stopped, Chuck stopped. If Ajax took two steps to the left, Chuck took two steps to the left. And the entire column of soldiers followed him like that, one by one, matching every move. At least, Chuck assumed that they did. That was a matter of faith too. Chuck couldn't turn around. He kept his eyes on his dog. He simply had to believe that everyone else was behind him, that he hadn't wandered off. That he and Ajax weren't all alone.

But there was nothing more lonesome than walking point in the jungles of Vietnam.

Although he knew that he had an entire platoon of soldiers behind him, in front of him, there was only green. The pale green of the elephant grass gave way to the deep green of trees and jungle bushes as the canopy rose overhead, turning the world into an endless emerald maze.

The shadows themselves seemed alive, ink-black monsters ready to swallow Chuck whole. If an attack came, it would hit him first. If Ajax missed a trap, Chuck would set it off before anyone else got there. His life could end before the soldiers behind him even knew anything was wrong. He'd never again smell that clean-laundry smell of his mother's wash hung up on the line; he'd never again bury his face in the soft fur on the back of his dog's neck. He'd never do anything, because he'd be dead in the jungle, far away from home. He would exist and then, *poof,* he wouldn't.

Every step he took felt like stepping to the edge of a cliff. His belly button tingled. Mud sucked at his boots.

The only way to go forward was to focus on Ajax. The dog stopped every few feet to sniff the air. At one point, he sniffed at the ground and then changed direction, walking to the right and up a small slope. Chuck followed, looking back and pointing so that the message would be passed down the line and someone could stop to investigate the possible booby trap.

It happened again ten minutes later, this time taking them in a wide arc around a cluster of trees. Chuck stopped to squat down and look. He squinted and made out a thin thread running along at the height of their toes. It was one of many lines weaving among the trees like a spider's web. He stayed still, following the first thread with his eyes, tracking it up a tree trunk to the mossy crook of a branch five feet off the ground.

The VC had hidden a claymore mine under the moss so that when a passing soldier hit the trip wires, it would blow up straight into his face, blasting out a wall of flame and sharp metal fragments, probably tearing the head off the first guy and gravely wounding anyone behind him. And that was just one of the threads. From what Chuck could tell, the spider's nest was hooked up to at least four other mines in the trees and who knew how many buried in the ground.

Chuck passed the signal down the line.

Ajax moved on, dodging a pit of punji stakes and two more trip wires in under an hour. They must have been close to an enemy position to encounter this many traps in such a small area. Chuck found himself forgetting to breathe, wondering when the first attack would come. Would the VC wait until they set off a trap, or would they tire of waiting and just open fire when Chuck took one step too many in their direction?

He asked himself as he stepped forward: Would this be the step that did it?

Or this one?

Or this one?

He stopped moving. He knew the line would stop behind him. But he just couldn't get his feet to take another step. After two years, one month, and fifteen days in Vietnam, after hundreds of patrols just like this one, he felt exhausted, a kind of tired that had nothing to do with the ache in his feet or the soreness in his muscles.

"What's up, Chuck?" Double O whispered behind him. "Ajax found something?"

Chuck didn't answer, just stared down at the ground in front of him. He pictured a helmet rolling away down a slope, a streak of blood left behind it in the mud. He shuddered at the memory.

Ajax looked back at him, panting. He cocked his head to the side with his big brown eyes wide, curious. He usually gave the signal to stop, after all, not his human handler. This was something new. He walked back to Chuck and pressed his nose against Chuck's leg, nuzzling at his side. He wanted to keep going. He wanted Chuck to be okay.

Ajax was ready for anything as long as Chuck was by his side. Ajax didn't let fear stop him in his tracks, didn't get lost in thoughts of danger. Ajax just walked until it was time to stop walking, and then he rested and then he did it all over again because that was what was asked of him. And that was what was asked of Chuck too.

He had to be like Ajax. The sooner he got moving, the sooner they could get out of the jungle and get back to base, where it was safe and there was ping-pong and maybe a letter from home. He just had to take the first step. And then the one after that, one at a time, until they were safe.

Ajax nudged him forward with his nose and Chuck took that first step.

"Good boy," Chuck told his dog.

He took the next step, and Ajax stayed right by his side. He kept stepping and he kept telling himself with each step, "I'm still okay. Just one more. I'm still okay. Just one more."

Like that, they walked on for an hour.

Suddenly, Ajax stopped. He wouldn't budge. Chuck tugged just to be sure, but Ajax had planted himself in place.

The hair rose on Ajax's back. He pressed his paws deep into the earth in front of him and pointed his nose forward. Then he looked back at Chuck. A scout dog wants his master to know when he's found something. He doesn't keep secrets. Ajax's muscles rippled with tension. And Chuck knew: This was it.

They'd found the enemy.

CHAPTER 5

FIREFIGHT

Chuck raised his fist up and the platoon behind him stopped and crouched, their weapons aimed all around to cover every possible direction of attack.

Chuck's breath felt hot and heavy in his lungs. Sticky like the napalm the air force dropped from their bombers. Liquid fire. His eyes darted through the trees, trying to figure out what Ajax smelled, trying to brace himself for an ambush.

"Perkins, what do we have?" Lieutenant Maxwell and his radioman crouched beside Chuck, whispering. Behind them Double O set his big machine gun on its tripod in the mud and pointed it past them. If the enemy came at the platoon from the front, Double O would cut them down with a rain of hot lead. The private next to him pulled out an ammo can, lifting a glistening belt of bullets at the ready. Each one was as long as a sharpened number-two pencil.

"Ajax alerted," Chuck whispered to the lieutenant. "By the look of his reaction, we've got something ahead. Nothing huge. Maybe four or five guys. Any more and Ajax'd be showing more signs."

The lieutenant nodded. He waved back at the line, signaling for the second squad to come forward. Billy Beans and the rest scampered to the front of the line, keeping their heads down and their guns ready. Sergeant Cody nodded gravely as Lieutenant Maxwell told him what he wanted. For once Ajax didn't even bother looking at the sergeant. He had bigger worries.

"Your squad's up to check it out," the lieutenant said. "Two teams, left and right flank, see what we've got."

Chuck felt his nerves calming down, even as they prepared to engage the enemy. He was no longer a lone scout creeping ahead through the jungle. He was part of a platoon getting ready for a fight. And he didn't have to go first into the attack. Ajax had done his job well.

"Good boy," Chuck whispered right into the dog's ear, giving him a rubdown along his side. Ajax wagged his tail, pleased with himself, but still his ears pointed skyward and his eyes scanned the trees. In this jungle, not even a big German shepherd could let his guard down.

Sergeant Cody picked five guys to go to the left with him and sent four the other way. They broke apart as they walked forward so that the platoon was laid out like a Y, with Chuck, Ajax, Double O and his gun, and Lieutenant Maxwell and his radioman at the intersection. Billy Beans gave Chuck a nervous smile as he passed and broke off in the smaller group to the right. Chuck nodded at Billy, and for some reason he didn't understand, gave the peace sign, two fingers in a V, like the hippies did.

Billy shook his head and chuckled, but his face turned serious the moment he looked away and focused back on the jungle before him. Somewhere out there, the enemy was lying in wait. Part of him hoped it was nothing, hoped that Ajax was wrong. Another part of him hoped that they'd find the enemy and that he'd get his first kill and maybe get put up for the Combat Action Ribbon. He wished he'd gone with the sergeant's group. The sergeant was the one who could recommend him for the ribbon. If they got into a fire-fight, he'd need to do something heroic, something to make sure he got noticed for his bravery.

He hoped he would be brave.

He had no way to be certain how he'd react until it happened. He'd heard of guys who froze up when the shooting started, tough guys who cried and cool guys who just ran away. Billy hoped he'd be a guy who could bring out the best in himself when it mattered. He'd been raised to believe there was no better test of a man than battle. He told himself he was ready to be tested.

The air smelled like mold and rot. His boots were caked with thick mud, he had an itch on the small of his back where sweat was trickling down, and mosquitoes buzzed in his ear and swarmed by his lips and his eyes. He kept having to swat them away. In his daydreams about the valor of combat, there were never this many little annoyances.

He looked around among the bushes and trees for footprints or any signs of an enemy campsite. It made him think about back home, hunting with his dad. The first time he'd ever gone hunting, the rifle had felt so big and heavy in his hands, even though it was just a little .22. His dad had taught him how to shoot, how to control his breathing and aim. How to squeeze the trigger without jerking the gun.

He tried to shoot a rabbit that he saw chewing on some grass — he'd always loved rabbit stew — but when he raised the gun, he couldn't pull the trigger. He was just a kid then, and the rabbit reminded him of Bugs Bunny. He couldn't shoot Bugs Bunny. The rabbit got away and his father had looked so disappointed. The memory of the shame made his ears blush.

But his father wasn't here now, and Billy wasn't hunting Bugs Bunny anymore.

"Beans!" The whisper cut into his thoughts, snapped him back. The guy behind him grabbed his shoulder and yanked him backward. "Pay attention, will ya? You're gonna get us all killed."

Billy looked down and saw that he'd been about to put his foot down on a trip wire. He wished Ajax had come up front with them. He looked at the soldier who'd stopped him, a black guy who hung out with Double O a lot. "Mose" or "Moose," they called him. Billy couldn't remember which, or why. The guy had just saved Billy's life. It was the first time they'd ever spoken.

Billy nodded his thanks, and they stepped over the trip wire and crept forward.

Time stretched out. Every second felt like an hour. It had only been five minutes since they'd split off from the rest of the platoon, but it felt like a lifetime ago. Billy swatted some big, buzzing thing off his ear.

All of sudden, he heard Ajax bark behind him. Billy stopped and looked back at Mose or Moose, who just shrugged. Ajax barked again, furiously, so Billy did the only thing he could think to do. He dropped to the ground.

What happened next happened fast.

As soon as Billy hit the ground, he heard a loud snap. He looked up and saw Mose or Moose stumble backward and fall. The tree behind him seemed to shred apart, and the snapping turned into a roar of machine-gun fire. The jungle lit up.

"Incoming!" someone yelled.

"I'm hit!" Mose or Moose yelled.

"Return fire, dammit!" the sergeant yelled.

Streaks of lightning zipped overhead as Double O unleashed his big gun in the direction of the enemy. Billy could see it tearing through the leaves and branches to his right. He turned in the direction that Double O's bullets were going, tucked his rifle into his shoulder, and even though he didn't know what he was shooting at, he opened fire on the jungle ahead of him.

The gun rattled his arm and roared as it spat fire. His blasts added to the amazing thunder of the battle, and Billy stopped thinking about Nancy back home or about getting a medal or a ribbon or shooting rabbits. He just squeezed his trigger and rained hell on whoever had the misfortune to be on the other side of the jungle from him.

A mortar shell crashed into a tree up above, exploding on impact and showering the ground below with sparks and flaming branches. The blue sky showed through in the gap where the treetop had once been.

Billy looked up at the tiny patch of blue, a skylight in the roof of jungle, and he smiled.

It felt good to be alive. He kept firing his gun into trees, and he kept smiling as he fired.

CHAPTER 6

DIGGING HOLES

"**H**old your fire!" Billy heard someone shouting. "Hold your fire!"

It was Sergeant Cody, his bright blond hair blazing beneath his helmet. Billy could see him moving ahead through the smoke to check out the status of their enemy. The overwhelming U.S. firepower had silenced the VC's guns, and it was time to assess the damage and count the kills. Billy exhaled a sigh of relief. He'd survived his first firefight . . . and he'd enjoyed it.

Mose — that was the guy's name, not Moose, Billy remembered — kept crying out. "Medic! I need a medic here!"

Doc Malloy scrambled through the trees and knelt down beside Mose, speaking comforting words to him and checking out his wounds.

"I think you'll be all right," he told Mose. "Bullet went clear through the flesh of your arm. Didn't even hit bone."

"Is it bad enough to get me out of 'Nam?" Mose asked.

Doc shook his head and patted Mose on the shoulder. "Sorry, brother. You'll be back in action in a few days."

Mose shook his head and sighed. "Charlie can't even shoot me proper. I'm never gettin' outta this war."

"We've got a blood trail!" the sergeant called from up ahead. "We need Ajax!"

Chuck and Ajax came tearing through the underbrush. The dog was panting like crazy and pulling Chuck forward. Double O was right behind.

Billy followed because he figured, how often do you get to see a scout dog hunt a person down?

When they reached Sergeant Cody, he was standing over a small puddle of blood on the jungle floor. It was already swarming with ants.

Chuck pointed, and Ajax stuck his nose right into the spot, snorting and pawing at the ants and pulling in quick bursts of air to get the scent.

"Ajax," Chuck said, and Ajax looked right up at him, his eyes wide and his jaw set. "Get him! Get him!" Chuck commanded, pointing into the jungle.

Ajax bounded off, both back legs pumping together, leaping over obstacles as Chuck hung on to the leash and followed right behind him. Billy Beans, Double O, and the sergeant followed too.

The lieutenant ordered Doc Malloy to go after them so he could look at the enemy's wounds if they caught him. He said that a prisoner could be an important source of intelligence, whatever that meant.

"Stay right behind me," Chuck called back. "There could still be booby traps out here."

Billy and Double O took care to step only where Chuck stepped, but Doc Malloy was about ten yards behind and struggling to catch up. He cursed under his breath as he picked his way through the jungle, doubting every step.

"Hurry up, Doc!" Chuck called back. "Ajax waits for no man!"

"I've always been a cat person," Doc panted as he caught up with the group standing in a semicircle around a small hole in the ground. Their guns were pointed down at the opening.

"Yeah, but I've never seen a cat do this," Chuck said, and unclipped Ajax from his leash.

The VC dug tunnels all over the country, a complicated

network of holes and tunnels, some of them big enough to be underground bases and hospitals, others barely big enough for one person. They used the tunnels to move around unseen and to hide weapons and food. They used the tunnels to disappear after an ambush, but there was no disappearing when Ajax was on the trail. They didn't dig tunnels deep enough to escape his nose.

The dog pounced on the small hole, wiggling his body inside and growling. Seconds later, they heard a scream as Ajax backed out of the opening, his tail rigid, his legs straining. When he got farther out, they saw that he held a man's forearm in his jaws and was dragging him up to the surface.

The man was screaming and struggling, but there wasn't enough room for him to bring his other arm around to push Ajax off. Not that he could have, anyway.

"Don't you dare hurt my dog," Chuck said as he pressed his boot down on the man's shoulder. Once he was half out of the hole, Chuck commanded Ajax *off*, and Sergeant Cody hauled the Vietcong soldier the rest of the way out. Double O and Billy kept their guns trained on the guy, but the fight had left him the moment he saw the Americans towering over him with their weapons. The ground where he'd been dragged was painted with blood.

Doc bent down and went to work immediately. The man didn't make another sound, just looked up at Doc with fear in his eyes.

"Will he live?" Lieutenant Maxwell had caught up with them and stood behind Doc, watching him work.

"We need a bird to medevac him out of here, but he'll live," said Doc.

"All right," said the lieutenant. "Let's clear a landing zone. Sergeant, have second squad do it, while the others get their foxholes dug around the perimeter. We'll spend the night here and medevac the prisoner out in the morning. Tie him to that tree over there."

"Hold on a second, sir," said Double O. "You telling me that Charlie tries to kill us, and he gets flown outta here on a chopper, while the rest of us have to dig in for the night?"

"Don't ask the lieutenant stupid questions," said the Beach Boy sergeant.

"It's okay," said Lieutenant Maxwell. "And yes, that is what I am telling you, specialist. So you better start digging."

"Shoot." Double O shook his head. "Maybe I should go fight for the VC. I'd get out of the jungle faster."

"Keep talking like that, and you'll get court-martialed out of this jungle," said Sergeant Cody.

"Maybe I'd rather be in jail back in the States than slogging around in this mess," answered Double O.

"Hey, Chuck," Billy called, stepping over to Chuck and Ajax. He didn't want to get caught up in the trouble Double O's mouth was about to get in. "Where you digging in?"

"I don't know yet," said Chuck.

"How about I dig your foxhole for you," Billy offered.

"You what?" Chuck asked.

The foxholes were pits as deep as a man, where the soldiers would sleep and keep lookout. If fighting started, they'd have the hole to take cover in and to shoot from. With a poncho stretched over the top, they were almost invisible too. When not walking or fighting, infantry grunts spent most of their time clearing away brush, digging these holes, and then filling them in again.

Digging a foxhole in the jungle mud was the most backbreaking work the army had ever dreamed up. Even Ajax looked at Billy funny, like the dog understood what a crazy offer he'd made.

"I just . . . you know." Billy rubbed the back of his neck and looked at his feet. "I figured if I dug your hole for you, next to mine . . . to say thanks for what Ajax did for me, barking like he did, before the ambush . . ."

"Just doing our job," said Chuck, rubbing Ajax behind the ears.

"Yeah," said Billy. "I know, but —"

"He don't want to dig your hole." Double O came over, shaking his head. He'd been dismissed by the lieutenant before he and Sergeant Cody could get into a screaming match.

"I just said that I did," said Billy. "And I say what I mean."

"Don't sound like it to me." Double O gave Billy the same sideways look that Ajax had. "My mama's a school-teacher, and she always told us to speak like a well-aimed bullet. Straight and true."

"You calling me a liar?" Billy balled his fists.

"Guys, calm down," Chuck interrupted their standoff. "You're making Ajax nervous. We got enough going on out here in the jungle without you two getting at each other's throats. I'll dig my own foxhole."

"Nah." Double O smiled a devious smile. "Billy's a man of his word. Right, Billy?"

"I am," said Billy, coolly.

"Except what he meant to say was that he'll dig *Ajax's* foxhole for him. Billy don't care if you there or not. He just wants that dog in the hole next to him in case there's a sneak attack tonight. And so do I. So I'll help him dig, as long as I get to dig in on the other side of you."

Chuck looked at Billy, and Billy shrugged. Double O was right. He didn't need to be such a jerk about it, but it was true. What if Charlie tried to sneak up on them in the night? The dog had saved his life with an early warning once already. He felt like his odds of getting home to Nancy Werner were a lot better if he stayed close to Ajax.

Chuck chuckled. He looked back and forth between Billy and Double O. Other guys on other combat patrols had made the offer to dig his foxhole before — these two weren't the first to feel safer around Ajax — but Chuck had never accepted the offer. He didn't think he should get special privileges because of Ajax. He was a soldier just like the rest of them, doing his job, following the rules.

But Chuck figured these two guys could use some time to work out their differences, and nothing bonds two people together better than hours of hard labor. Also, Chuck was exhausted. It had been a heck of a day, and tomorrow probably wouldn't be any better.

While Double O and Billy dug his foxhole, Chuck and Ajax checked the rest of the area for booby traps and then played a rough-and-tumble game of tug-of-war with an old rope tied to a can. Ajax couldn't get enough of that toy. The wag of his tail and his gleeful grunts made carrying the extra weight worthwhile.

As they played, the prisoner tied to the tree watched them closely, his face an expressionless mask. If he was angry or afraid, it was impossible to tell. If Chuck were in his place, he'd be angry and he'd be afraid. The Americans were foreigners here, just like the French before them. Vietnam had been at war for so long, it was a wonder anyone had any will left to fight at all. But that was the problem, wasn't it?

For the Vietnamese it wasn't about having the will to fight. This was their country. For them, there was no end to a tour of duty and there was no retreat. They couldn't just go home, because they were home. The war was their home.

Yeah, Chuck thought, he'd be angry. But the prisoner just stared, didn't show any emotion at all, and his gaze quickly drained all the fun out of playing with Ajax. Chuck took his dog over to watch Double O and Billy Beans dig their foxholes, and then they all settled in for the long, wet night.

The rain plopped down on the leaves of the canopy above them and splattered on the mud around them. The wind rustled branches and bushes, and everything sounded like an ambush about to start, like the jungle itself was the enemy. Their minds all conjured phantoms beyond their foxholes.

"Tell me the truth," Billy whispered to Chuck across the darkness. "Did you really volunteer to stay over two years in this mess for a dog?"

Chuck thought a moment, considering how to answer. "He's not just a dog," he said. "He's my partner."

"He a good dog," Double O whispered on the other side of Chuck. "But he ain't good enough to make me stay in this hellhole one minute longer than I need to."

"I got assigned to work with Ajax in February 1968 with the Fiftieth Infantry Scout Dog Platoon," Chuck explained. It was so dark out he didn't even need to close his eyes to picture it. The guys on either side of him listened quietly to his voice, barely loud enough to hear over the plunking rain.

"We guarded outposts and walked point on patrols, searching for booby traps and for enemies waiting in ambush.

He was a good dog, and we did our job just fine. I was a short-timer, only had two months left in my deployment, when I was sent with the air cavalry into the Ia Drang Valley."

Neither Billy nor Double O knew what the Ia Drang Valley was, but they knew that a short-timer — a soldier with just a few weeks left in Vietnam — was usually spared the most dangerous missions. Usually, but not always.

"An entire North Vietnamese battalion came down on us almost as soon as we dismounted in the valley," Chuck said, picturing it like a movie playing on the darkness in front of his eyes. "They cut us off from our reinforcements and then spent the next two days and nights picking us apart. I took a bullet in the thigh and fell, just as Charlie overran our position. Explosions all around us, the air thick with lead. I saw my buddy Lou lying nearby and I crawled over to him, tried to jostle him. Soon as I did, his helmet fell off and rolled down a little mud embankment. His head was still in it as it rolled away. His body twitched, like it didn't know it'd lost the most important part. You couldn't hear your own thoughts over the sound of machine-gun fire and heavy artillery. I saw splinters of bone stuck inches deep into tree trunks, blown there by land mine explosions. Ajax was scared. I didn't have him on a leash, and he could have run away. It's in a dog's instinct to run. Heck, I wanted to run. But Ajax didn't run. He stayed by my side, standing over me while I lay bleeding in the mud.

"That's when this little guy came out of the bush, running at me, holding an old rifle, like something from World War I. It had a bayonet on the tip. It looked huge in his hands, much too big for him, and he lowered it and charged. I knew that was it for me. I was dead. This little man was going to run me through, not even waste a bullet on me. I whispered a prayer; I'm not sure now what it was. I'd never paid much attention in Sunday School. I don't know if God was listening to me, but I know that Ajax was.

"He jumped between me and the VC, jumped over the bayonet, and took the man down by the throat. I got the gun and used it as a crutch, holding onto Ajax's collar with my other hand. Ajax led me out of that jungle and back to the landing zone for the medevac chopper. I owe that dog my life. I promised him then that I'd never leave him behind, just like he didn't leave me. I looked him in those big brown eyes and I promised.

"When my tour was up a few weeks later, I knew Ajax couldn't leave with me. He's classified as military equipment, you know? They don't release military equipment while there's a war on. But a promise is a promise. So I reenlisted for another six months. Served by his side. The war kept going. Uncle Sam wasn't ready to let Ajax go, so I reenlisted again. Six more months. And then I did it again after that. I've been in-country for two years, one month, and, well, sixteen days now. I guess I'll keep doing it until the war's over and Ajax and I can go home."

"Four tours." Double O whistled in the dark. "You are one loyal Devil Dog, Chuck. Crazy. But loyal."

"I must take after Ajax then," he answered.

"Guess so," said Double O.

"I'm glad you stayed on," said Billy. "Real glad."

They fell silent again, listening to the night and trying to ignore their worries. Even though it was pitch-black, Chuck knew that every soldier in the platoon, from the two guys on either side of him to Doc in his tent behind them and the lieutenant across the landing zone, was listening anxiously through the rain and the wind for any sound from Ajax.

A bark could be the only warning they would have of an attack.

In his foxhole, Chuck thought about Lou and Ia Drang. He thought about all those days on point and all those nights just as dark and bleak as this one. Two years, one month, and sixteen days. The only thing between him and seventeen days was the jungle night ahead. He held Ajax close against his chest and listened, just like the others. The night roared around them, but Ajax was calm.

CHAPTER 7

OUR GIVEN NAMES

Early the next morning, the chopper came. It touched down on the landing zone and the Beach Boy sergeant hustled the prisoner on to it. Mose climbed on with his arm in a sling and gave the peace sign to the guys staying behind. He was smiling, glad to be getting out of the bush, even though he knew he'd be going back as soon as he was healed.

In under a minute, the helicopter lifted off again, whipping the trees into a whirlwind as it went. The slap of its rotors on the air faded into a memory, and the platoon was alone in the jungle again.

Chuck and Ajax stood with Doc by the foxholes while Double O and Billy filled them in again with dirt and mud.

"Why do they call you Billy Beans?" asked Chuck.

"'Cause he a bean farmer back in Nowheresville,'" laughed Double O.

"I'm from just outside Minneapolis," said Billy. "It's not nowhere."

"I'm from New York City," said Double O. "Everywhere else is nowhere."

"Even here?"

"Especially here," said Double O. "Now tell the Devil Dog about your nickname. He never gonna believe it."

Billy blushed. "I got it back at the replacement center in Saigon," he said. "When they gave me my box of rations, it was all beans, nothing but cans of beans. I couldn't live on just beans, so I asked the major in charge of the post if I could, you know, trade."

"You asked an army major about trading beans?" Chuck laughed. He'd never even spoken to a major.

"I did." Billy laughed with him. "He got right in my face and said, 'You don't *like* beans? You want to trade like kids at the school cafeteria? You want to trade your beans for my brownies, Private, is that it? Or do you think I look like a lunch lady? Do you see a hairnet on me?' And I said, 'No, sir, I don't see a hairnet, sir, I just have too many beans, sir . . .'"

"And that was that," said Double O.

"And that was that," agreed Billy. "The major told the captains and the lieutenants and the sergeants, and pretty soon everyone knew and I was Billy Beans."

"How about your name, Double O?" asked Chuck.

"I gave it to myself. I'm the black James Bond. Like 007, but so slick I don't need a number, just the double *oh*s."

"Doc's easy," said Billy.

"Back home they called me Dozer because I was a bull-dozer on the football field," said Doc.

"Not Jell-O?" joked Double O. "You know, 'cause you a bit jiggly?"

Doc scowled.

"All right, let's roll," Lieutenant Maxwell called out. The men pulled themselves together, stuffing supplies back into their rucksacks, shoving food into their faces, and slapping helmets onto their heads. They took formation with Chuck and Ajax in the lead, and stepped off again on their march to the river.

They left behind empty ration cans of beans and meat-balls and peaches and one empty can of dog food. The holes they'd filled in quickly turned to mud. The landing zone, the foxholes, and even their garbage would be consumed by jungle in a matter of weeks, and forgotten.

Ajax snuffled at the dirt, paused to lift his leg against a tree, and led them on. They found no other traps and Ajax didn't alert to any other ambushes. To everyone's surprise, the day passed without enemy contact at all. It was wet and hot, but they made good time. That night, Billy and Double O dug Chuck's hole again and again they all spent the night half-awake, listening for a warning bark from the bright-eyed German shepherd.

"You grow up with dogs, Chuck?" Billy whispered in the dark.

"Nope," said Chuck. "Never had a dog. I always wanted one. That's why I signed up for the scout dog unit. Figured if my mom wouldn't let me get a dog, good old Uncle Sam and his army would. And look at me now, huh?"

"I grew up with dogs," said Billy. "Hunting dogs, mostly. How about you, Double O?"

"Huh?" Double O answered, groggy. "You asking about dogs?"

"Yeah," said Billy.

"We had subway rats the size of dogs, if that's what you mean," said Double O.

"No dogs?" asked Billy.

"There was a junkyard dog near my grandma's house. Mean beast. Racist too."

"A dog can't be racist," said Billy. "They don't know how to hate."

"Oh, you wrong there, Billy," said Double O. "Everything travels right down that leash, from master to canine. Man to dog. Dogs can be racist if the people around 'em are racist."

"So you think Ajax don't like Vietnamese people?" asked Billy.

"I think Ajax doesn't like anyone who doesn't like me," said Chuck. "Race has nothing to do with it."

"Ah," Double O sighed in the dark. "That's easy for you to say."

"What is?" asked Chuck.

"Saying that race has nothing to do with it. Not your fault, of course. You were born how you were born, just like me, but you can forget about race whenever you feel like it. That's the white man's privilege. Not me or the other brothers. Not the Vietnamese. We get reminded that we ain't the white man just about every day, get it?"

"I get it," said Chuck.

They fell silent again, listening to the night, thinking about what Double O said.

Chuck was glad to share his foxhole with Ajax, to keep the dog close. Race, politics, all that stuff didn't matter to the dog. Did he have enough to eat? Was he safe? Was it time to play? The simple questions drove his life, and they all had yes or no answers. Chuck wished everything could have a yes or no answer. There was a reason dogs slept so well, and Chuck figured it had a lot to do with that.

The soldiers woke to the third day of their patrol eager to get to the river and get airlifted back to their outpost.

"Check yourselves for leeches," Doc Malloy warned everyone. "You don't want those bloodsuckers feeding on you all day." To prove his point, he used his utility knife to pry a fat black leech from the side of his neck. It had slithered onto him in the night and gorged itself on his blood. It hit the ground with a moist plop and Doc squashed it under his boot.

The guys cringed, but they all checked themselves for leeches.

Chuck triple-checked Ajax, who was already panting with anticipation for the day. He loved a walk in the jungle.

Dogs didn't worry about leeches, so Chuck had to worry for him.

"I heard about a grunt up by the Laos border who had a leech crawl right up his privates," said Billy Beans.

"You sick." Double O shook his head. "That's sick."

"It's true," said Billy. "Heard it from my cousin in the Marine Corps. Guy in his battalion saw it happen. The poor sucker had to be flown to Japan for surgery to have the leech removed from . . . you know . . . down there."

Double O laughed. Billy could always be counted on to believe any crazy story he heard. He wasn't worth getting angry at. Billy was dumb as a brick, but good for entertainment.

They walked for hours. The jungle grew thick with tangled roots and a squad had to come forward to hack at it with their machetes so they could keep going. Ajax led them safely past two more booby traps. They hit the river in late afternoon, and the lieutenant called in the airlift.

"I got some good news for you." He came over to Chuck and Ajax, smiling. Ajax had his snout shoved into a can of dog food, chowing down, while Chuck leaned against a burned tree stump and watched the river. He stood when

Lieutenant Maxwell approached, but he didn't salute. Enemy snipers could be watching, and they would have loved to take out an officer.

Billy and Double O glanced over, listening in.

"Looks like you're out of the bush," said Lieutenant Maxwell.

"Excuse me, sir?" Chuck asked.

"I got orders that you're flying back to the Fiftieth Scout Dog Platoon today. Too bad. We'll miss you. You've done great work with us out here. Ajax saved a lot of lives. You should be proud."

"We are, sir." Chuck smiled. "I can't take credit, though. Ajax is the best there is. I hope we'll get assigned to your platoon again before this is all done with."

"You don't understand, Chuck," said Lieutenant Maxwell. "You won't be assigned to *any* platoon again. The Fiftieth Scout Dog Platoon is pulling out."

Chuck felt the earth shift beneath his feet. He felt light-headed. "Sir?" was all he could muster.

"All the infantry scout dog platoons are pulling out," the lieutenant explained. "The South Vietnamese army is taking over. I'm sure the rest of us will be going home soon after you."

Chuck felt like he had slipped into a dream. Nothing felt real. The wind off the river, the rustle of the mangrove trees, the call of nervous birds in the canopy, none of it made any sense to him. He couldn't be leaving. He'd been in-country so long, it was all he knew. He looked down at Ajax, who looked right back up at him, licking his black doggy lips.

"You ready to go home, boy?" the lieutenant asked the dog, but Ajax didn't react at all. Maybe he didn't respond to voices other than his master's, or maybe he didn't have any idea what the word *home* could mean, but he just kept staring up at Chuck, who stood unmoving on the riverbank as the water rushed by.

CHAPTER 8

HOME, BUT NOT SO SWEET

The Fiftieth Infantry Scout Dog Platoon was home away from home for fifteen dogs and their handlers. They had a small barracks, a cluster of sandbag-ringed defensive positions, a headquarters building, and a dog kennel with an obstacle course for training, all tucked away in a quiet corner of a big base that housed thousands of other soldiers, an entire combat brigade. Chuck liked spending time with the other dog handlers. They never asked him why he kept reenlisting for more tours of duty.

Each dog team came and went from this base to attach to different units for a time, until their assigned mission was done or they couldn't do their mission anymore. The higher-ups usually left the scout dog platoon to itself, so it wasn't a bad place to spend the war, except that it didn't have a ping-pong table. The little outpost where he'd left his mark in the tree was a long helicopter flight away, and he guessed he'd never see it again.

When Chuck came into the barracks, Griffin, a red-headed sergeant who was on his second tour in Vietnam, lay on his cot with no shirt on. He didn't look up as Chuck tossed his pack down onto his own cot. He was throwing a chewed-up baseball into the air and catching it again. His dog tags rested on his chest next to the scar he'd gotten from an enemy grenade thrown into his foxhole a few months back. His first dog, Champ, hadn't survived the attack. His new German shepherd, Bruno, was snoozing across his feet at the end of the cot, his paws twitching as he dreamed.

"Where's Ajax?" Griffin asked.

"Back in the kennel, asleep," said Chuck. "Heck of a patrol. First day, we couldn't go ten yards without a trip wire and then had some serious contact with the VC. After that, two long days of nothing. Just boots and mud, and suddenly I'm sent back here, told the Fiftieth is done. What's that about?"

"I hear they might give you a medal," said Griffin.

Chuck shrugged. He wasn't in this war to pin shiny medals to his chest.

"I'm serious about the medal." Griffin caught the baseball with a hard smack into his palm. Bruno opened his eyes to consider it for a moment, then went back to sleep. The big dog had a reputation for being lazy. Platoons groaned when they saw Griffin and Bruno sent out with them. He could make a patrol take twice as long because he needed to rest all the time. But the laziness wasn't Bruno's fault. German shepherds just weren't meant to work in the wet jungle heat. Neither were people, for that matter, but here they were.

"I heard Lieutenant Stockman on the radio with that platoon lieutenant, Maxwell," Griffin said. "He was saying how you saved their lives, stopped an ambush, and recovered a fleeing prisoner. Says you should get the Bronze Star. What do you think of that?"

Chuck didn't know. If anyone deserved the Bronze Star, it was Ajax. Chuck was just the guy at the other end of the leash. He repeated his question. "What'd I hear about the Fiftieth pulling out? Are we going home?"

"Sure are," Griffin sighed. "Back to the world. Home sweet home, where the only explosions are on the Fourth of July."

"What about our dogs?" Chuck asked, ignoring what Griffin thought of as humor.

Griffin didn't answer. The corners of his mouth twitched.

"What? Tell me." Chuck stepped over to Griffin's cot, towered above him.

"They're classified as military equipment," Griffin said. "Like generators or artillery or —"

"Yeah, I know all that," Chuck cut him off.

"The generals have made a decision," Griffin sighed. "The cost of shipping certain military equipment back to the States is too high to make it worthwhile. We're leaving our generators behind, some artillery, and —"

"No." Chuck's stomach felt like a heavy stone sinking in a cold pond. "The dogs are getting shipped to other bases or something? Guard duty in Okinawa? Something."

"Morris will check them all out," said Griffin, sadly. Morris was the platoon veterinary technician. "Some of the dogs who are still fit will be turned over for service with the ARVN."

ARVN stood for the Army of the Republic of Vietnam, the South Vietnamese army, who were the American's allies in the war against the Vietcong and the North Vietnamese Army.

Chuck sat down on his cot and let his head fall into his hands. "What does the ARVN know about dogs? They eat them!"

"That's just a rumor," said Griffin. "I've been on ARVN bases. Never eaten dog."

"That you know of," said Chuck, bitterly. "Anyway, what do they know about *caring* for dogs? There's not even a word in Vietnamese for *veterinarian*!"

Griffin looked at Bruno, sleeping. He set the ball down next to Bruno's nose and watched the black folds twitch at the end of his snout, the scent of the toy working its way into his dreams. Dogs never stopped smelling, even in their sleep.

Chuck's throat was dry. He looked up at Griffin. "And the ones they don't give away?"

Griffin just shook his head.

"Put down?" Chuck's voice cracked.

Griffin nodded. "They can't risk them bringing back weird jungle diseases to the U.S."

"I'm not letting that happen," said Chuck. "I won't."

"Morris has orders. He's sick about it."

"What's the lieutenant say?"

"Stockman's a career officer," said Griffin. "He wants a promotion to captain. He's not going to make waves on behalf of some surplus military equipment."

"I'm going to talk to him. He can't do this."

"What choice does he have?"

74

"These dogs saved our lives." Chuck stood. "Mine. Yours. More GIs than I can count. They've been through hell doing it, the heat and the damp and the long humps through the jungle. And they never signed up for this. They didn't *choose* to be here."

"They're dogs, man," said Griffin. "They don't choose anything. It's not like they plan for the future or nothing. All we can do is take care of 'em while they're alive and comfort them when they go."

"No!" said Chuck. "That's not good enough, not for Ajax. *He* deserves a Bronze Star, not to be put down like some kind of rabid mutt."

Griffin exhaled slowly. "Chuck, it's done. The generals have made the call. You're a fart's width above the rank of private. There's nothing you can do."

"I'm going to talk to Stockman. And Morris. I'll talk to the colonel and the generals if I have to. Nobody's putting Ajax down, and nobody's handing him over for stew."

"We lose them all eventually," Griffin said. "You know that. You're not going to change a thing. Not in this war."

"No!" Chuck snapped, like he was scolding a bad dog. Bruno even woke up to look questioningly at him. Chuck looked down at Griffin. "Champ's death wasn't your fault," he said. "But Bruno's will be if you just sit there and do nothing."

"Don't you dare," Griffin said as he shot to his feet, fists clenched. Bruno sat up on the bed, his ears perked up. He growled at Chuck. Chuck looked from one to the other and backed away toward the door, holding his palms out in a gesture of surrender.

He didn't want to fight Griffin and Bruno.

He wanted to fight the generals and the politicians, the men in the shiny shoes who'd never slept in a foxhole, who'd never counted on a four-legged fur ball with a cheerful grin to pull them out of the bush alive, to keep them alive through a thousand muddy miles. Men who would never know what real loyalty meant.

Ajax was not "surplus military equipment." Ajax was a soldier, and he was a great one. If the enemy killed him, well, that was a risk all soldiers faced. But Chuck hadn't stayed in Vietnam for two years, one month, and nineteen days just to let Ajax get put down by the people he trusted.

Chuck stormed out of the barracks, looking for Lieutenant Stockman. He'd made a promise never to leave his dog, and he was going to keep it.

CHAPTER 9

BAD TIMES

It was a bad time. Lieutenant Stockman shook his head and apologized, so Chuck went to see Colonel Guinsler.

Colonel Guinsler said there was nothing to be done.

Vet Tech Morris wept, openly, right in front of Chuck, and he pleaded for forgiveness, but he was going to do what he'd been told to do. He was going to ship some dogs off to the ARVN and he was going to put down the rest.

"I have to, Chuck," he said. "I hate to do it, but I have my orders."

"Refuse the order," Chuck told him. "Just refuse it."

"And get court-martialed?" Morris said. "Thrown in jail? I've got a wife. Did you know that? I want to see her again. The sooner this is done, the sooner I can go home to see her.

The sooner you can go home too. I know you've been in-country a while, Chuck, but this ain't your home."

"They trust you," Chuck said. "Every one of these dogs trusts you. Hell, Bruno doesn't like *anyone* and he likes you. And Ajax . . . You've wrestled with him, what, how many times? He'd never let anyone but me wrestle with him before he met you. He did his job, he served with honor. He followed the rules. How can you do this to him?"

"Better it's me than someone who doesn't care, right?" Morris sniffled and wiped his nose on his sleeve.

Somewhere in the jungle, out past the barbed wire, a monkey screeched. Right and left, guys were hauling crates and packing up supplies. One guy dropped a box of rations, and cans of beans and peaches and chili spilled all over the ground, rolling away from him. He cursed and chased after them. The Fiftieth Infantry Scout Dog platoon was taking itself apart all around them, but Chuck just stared at Morris.

At that moment, Chuck hated the veterinary technician. In fact, he hated Vietnam and everyone in it. He hated the war and everyone who wasn't in the war too. He hated everyone who was for the war and everyone who was against it. At that moment, he hated every human on earth. He hated himself too. He couldn't do anything to save Ajax from the machinery of the army, from its very human cruelty.

His head felt hot. His eyes pulsed. He gnashed his teeth. No one was as kind and good and loyal as they should be. No one would stand up for Ajax. Everyone just followed the rules, just like Chuck always had. But how could he follow this rule? How could he obey an order to turn his best friend over to be killed? But how could he disobey? He hardly even knew how.

He spat on the ground at Morris's feet and stormed off toward the kennels to hold his dog as close as he could hold him, just like he had in the foxhole.

The days passed in a blur of soldiers coming and going. The war had its own rhythms, and in spite of Chuck's despair, the beat went on. He spent all his waking hours in the kennels with Ajax, talking to him, grooming him, playing, and training.

He let Ajax eat extra rations of dog food. He let him try some of the human rations too — canned meatloaf and chili — but Ajax didn't seem to go for them. Tabasco sauce made him sneeze and lick his snout, which made Chuck fall over laughing.

Whenever one of the other handlers would come into the kennel to take his dog outside, Chuck and Ajax would watch them in silence. Sometimes the handlers looked like guys did before a patrol — jaws locked, eyes set forward, faces betraying no emotion. Sometimes the handlers looked like guys did after a patrol — eyes sunken with exhaustion, shaking hands, and wobbly feet.

"Hey, Chuck," they'd say.

"Hey," Chuck would say back.

One by one they came and took their dogs, and then they came back alone.

Chuck started sleeping in the kennels, right beside Ajax. The others let him be. He'd been in-country longer than any of them. But the day would come when it was his turn. He knew it. They all knew it.

Lieutenant Maxwell's platoon came back from their outpost in the hills and Chuck didn't go out to greet them. Griffin brought in a message that some of the grunts wanted to see him.

"They hauled some raggedy ping-pong table out with them," Griffin said. "A medic and some grunt named Beans, and a specialist called Double O. What kind of names are those?"

Chuck just grunted. "It wasn't their ping-pong table to move," he said. "I won. They should have left it by our tree."

"What tree?" Griffin squatted down beside him. Ajax let out a low growl and Griffin smiled sadly at the dog.

"Never mind," said Chuck.

Griffin went to get Bruno from his cage and spoke to his dog in whispers that Chuck and Ajax couldn't hear. Then they left together and they didn't come back. Another day passed. Or maybe it didn't.

Grief did that. Sadness tugged at the thread of time until it unraveled like a sweater. It either slowed down or sped up. Or sped down and slowed up. Chuck wasn't sure. There was only the present anyway, only he and Ajax. Chuck felt like he was living in dog years. Nothing but now. Except now went so fast.

When Lieutenant Maxwell came by the half-empty kennels for a hello–good-bye type of thing, Chuck didn't even bother to salute the young officer, a disobedience he never would have deliberately shown before. Chuck knew he was sitting on the floor of a kennel on a military base, dressed in his jungle camouflage, but in his mind, he was no longer a part of this army. It was the army's rules that made Ajax into a thing that could be put down, and Chuck didn't want any part of those rules.

He kept grooming Ajax, making the dog's black-and-brown coat smooth. It shined like a general's boots.

"I put you up for the Bronze Star," the lieutenant said, trying to make small talk.

Chuck grunted and kept brushing. Ajax panted in the afternoon heat. As soon as he was clean, he'd roll onto his back, kicking his four legs in the air and pressing himself into the dirt of the floor, covering himself with filth again. He was a jungle dog. He didn't like to be clean.

"Lieutenant Stockman asked me to come by," Lieutenant Maxwell said.

Chuck shrugged.

"We owe you our lives," Lieutenant Maxwell said. "You're a good soldier. A damn good soldier. But this —" He made a broad gesture that included Chuck and Ajax and the kennel. "This is no way to end an honorable tour. Four tours. You've got to pull yourself together."

Chuck didn't answer. Lieutenant Maxwell left. Lieutenant Stockman came by and said most of the things Lieutenant Maxwell had said. Sergeant Cody came by. He repeated what both the lieutenants had said, but he did it with more curse words. It was hard to take him seriously. Ajax kept growling at him. The sergeant was holding back tears as he cursed at Chuck to pull himself together.

Chuck dozed off. He dreamed of a big piece of land back in the States, a big ranch where he and Ajax could run — no leashes, no land mines, no orders. No rules. Just a guy and his dog and the sun and the grass.

But he woke with a start. It was dark in the kennel, but something had disturbed the darkness. His combat reflexes kicked in. His hand gripped his utility knife. Adrenaline raced up his spine. Beside him, Ajax sat up, wide awake, alert. He growled.

Someone was there.

CHAPTER 10

A KNIGHT'S QUEST

Was it time? Had they come to take Ajax away?

Chuck could fight. If he fought, he could slow them down. But he knew they'd win. They'd win in the end. He'd go to jail, and Ajax would still be put down, and the dog's last moments on earth would be filled with anger and fear, and Chuck wouldn't be there to help him through it. Ajax would be all alone when he needed his friend most.

Or he could do like Griffin said: take care of Ajax now, comfort him until the end. Stay by his side as his eyes closed and stroke his fur and let him go with dignity. Chuck couldn't fight the US Army. All he could do was give Ajax some peace. The dog had earned some peace, after all.

He had to decide.

They were here for him.

It was fight or let them take Ajax.

"You can't take him." Chuck stood and spoke into the darkness. "You can't just stick a needle in him. Not now. Not tonight."

"Ain't no needle sticking in nowhere," the darkness answered. Double O stepped from the shadows, with Billy Beans and Doc Malloy behind him. "Ajax ain't going out like *that*."

Billy smiled. "Hi, Chuck."

"We heard how they doin' Ajax," Double O said. "And we heard how you were takin' it, and, well . . . Doc had an idea."

"It's not really an idea," Doc Malloy explained. "I just had a thought, and Double O took it and had one of his . . . plans."

"It was my idea," said Billy Beans. "Double O had the plan, but I had the idea that started the plan."

"Yes, true," said Doc Malloy. "This madness has two fathers, and I'm not one of them."

"Don't be modest, Doc," Double O said. "You planted the seed. And the seed be growin'."

"I thought your mom was a teacher, Double O," said Billy. *"The seed be growin'?"*

"Just because I know the white man's rules doesn't mean I have to follow them."

"But you're always correcting me."

"Because you the white man. If you can't speak your own language, it's just sad."

Chuck and Ajax watched them argue, their heads moving side to side like they were watching a ping-pong match. Chuck still had no idea what this thought or idea or plan was or what it had to do with him or why these men had come all the way across the base to wake Chuck up from his dream and argue in front of him about it.

"Gentlemen," Doc interrupted. "Back to the matter at hand?"

"Right," said Double O. "So, we heard that you were rotating out and that the dogs weren't going with you. And that's when Doc had his . . . *thought*."

"All I did was mention that it was too bad there was no local place that could take them in," said Doc. "Back in the States, we have this organization, the ASPCA, that takes in abandoned dogs. I wished there was something like that here in Vietnam."

"But there's not," said Chuck. "There's nothing like that here." He looked at Ajax, the sharpness of his ears and snout,

86

the intelligence in his eyes. The love. Chuck didn't know how to let him die. Chuck didn't know how he could bear it and go on living.

"Well, that's when I had the idea," said Billy, his voice swollen with pride. "I heard from my cousin about a Frenchman up by the border."

"A Frenchman?" Chuck asked.

"Like I told you, my cousin's in the marines," said Billy. "And he told me about a patrol from his company that went up by the border with Laos, like, four months ago. A week in the bush, real hairy times. They fought through for days, and suddenly, they come out and they see this mansion. Like . . . like a real mansion. White columns and ivy and stained glass. Marble floors. And there's this Frenchman who owned the place. It was a rubber plantation when this was all a French colony. His family had it for generations. Way out on the edge of nowhere, and the guy never heard that the French got kicked out of Vietnam. He'd stayed on in his crazy mansion, eating off china plates and drinking out of crystal goblets and all that. He invited the marines in, like he was inviting them to tea. The guy was nuts."

"You're nuts for believing this story," said Doc. "It's make-believe. It's a Hollywood fantasy."

"But the dogs are the thing." Billy kept going, like he didn't hear Doc at all. "My cousin says the guy had, like, twenty dogs, all different kinds. Hunting dogs and lap dogs and those crazy little Vietnamese dogs we seen around."

"We *have* seen around," corrected Double O. "Past-perfect tense."

"Whatever," said Billy. "My point is, the marines asked this crazy old man why he had so many dogs, and he said that he was saving them. He was trying to show some civilized ways to the locals. Like if the Vietnamese could just save the dogs, there'd be no war and they'd all be rich, living in mansions and drinking from crystal goblets."

"You really shouldn't believe everything you hear," said Doc. "False hope is no hope at all."

Chuck cleared his throat. The story was crazy. There was no way it could be true. No way. But he didn't agree with Doc. Hope was hope. "So the guy is running a dog rescue out there in the bush, that's what you're saying?"

"That's why Double O came up with his plan," Billy said.

Double O nodded. "Simple, really," he said. "We take Ajax up there. Take him to the Frenchman."

"There is no Frenchman," said Doc.

"There is," said Billy. "If my cousin says there is, then there is. I mean, I've got the letter right here." He reached into his pocket and pulled out a moldy letter, half-rotten from the jungle, and waved it in Chuck's face. Double O pushed Billy's wrist down and looked Chuck square in the eyes.

"You know me, Chuck," said Double O. "I ain't one to believe Billy's stories. And I ain't one to take crazy risks. But I owe that dog my life, same as you do. All of us. So, I figure it's worth a shot. You're on your way to a Bronze Star or to the loony bin by the looks of it, but no matter what, you're out of this army soon enough. And, well, this was never my war. So I'm ready to go if you say you want to."

"Me too," said Billy. "I'm with Ajax."

"And Doc?" Chuck asked.

"It's a fool's quest." Doc shrugged. "But even fools need a medic, I guess," he added.

"So it's your call, Devil Dog," said Double O.

Chuck looked at Ajax panting beside him, the empty ration cans strewn about the kennel. There was nothing for him here. Nothing for him left in this army. If this place was real, if this Frenchman existed, he could leave Ajax there until the war was over.

Once there was peace — and there would have to be someday; all wars ended sometime — then he could come back and pick up his dog, take him back to the States, get that piece of land, let Ajax enjoy his retirement. If this Frenchman existed . . . It was a big if, a mansion in the jungle.

He thought about that book he'd read, *Don Quixote*, where the crazy guy goes off on a crazy quest. It was all about nobility and honor in a time when there wasn't enough of either.

"Quixotic," said Doc.

"Quick-what?" said Billy.

"Quixotic," said Doc. "That's the word Chuck's looking for." He looked at Chuck. "From that book you were reading up on the outpost. *Don Quixote*. A mad quest for some dreamed-up idea is called *quixotic*. And that's what these guys are suggesting. A quixotic quest."

"Quixotic," Chuck repeated, nodding. "I'm going to do it. But you guys don't need to come. If I run off, they won't make such a fuss. But if you guys go . . . You've got time left on your tours. They'll lock you up as deserters."

"Details," said Double O. "Just details."

"No," said Chuck, standing, brushing himself off. "That's not just details. It's your lives. I can't have you throw them away for me and Ajax."

"Ajax and I," corrected Billy.

"No," Double O said. "Chuck was right. Me and Ajax."

"You send me in the right direction, and I'll find the Frenchman," said Chuck. "You can't risk your futures for me." He shook his head. "No way."

"It ain't for *you*," said Double O, shaking his head right back at Chuck. "It's for Ajax. He was drafted just like us. They'd put us down just as soon as they'd put him down. And, like I said, Ajax ain't going down like that. Not on my watch."

"You all feel this way?" Chuck looked from man to man. They each nodded in turn, even Doc Malloy.

"Guys, I can't ask . . ." His voice caught in his throat. Chuck felt himself filling up, swelling with feelings he didn't know he could still feel, a crazy mixture of fear and gratitude and hope.

"You ain't askin'," said Double O. "We tellin' you. And now we got work to do. We gotta pack for about a week in the bush, I think, and we can't get caught packing. And then we gotta get past the sentries and get outside the wire. And that's when we're in it. No friends. No allies. VC and Uncle Sam both gunning for us. We'll need you and Ajax at your best."

"Oh, you'll have our best. But there's one thing." Chuck patted Ajax on the head. The dog looked up at him. His tail wagged slightly, sweeping the floor behind him, expectant. "We have to leave tonight."

The other guys looked at one another, eyebrows raised. Double O whistled. Billy cleared his throat.

"Look around," said Chuck. "The kennel's almost empty and the platoon's almost packed up. We'll be pulling out any day now, and Ajax's turn will come before that. It could come tomorrow. If you want to help me save him, we've got to do it tonight."

"Well, gentlemen." Doc clapped his hands together. "We've got about four hours until sunrise, so if we're going to commit this act of defiance against the United States Army, to which we've all pledged our loyalty, I suggest we start gathering our things."

They all nodded, and Chuck bent down to Ajax's level and looked him in the eyes. Ajax did what dogs do; he looked at his master and then he looked away and then he licked Chuck's face.

"You ready, pal?" Chuck whispered, pressing his mouth to Ajax's ear. "You ready to go AWOL, old friend?"

Ajax looked at Chuck like he understood, although he couldn't possibly understand.

AWOL.

Absent without leave.

Desertion.

It was a criminal act, punishable by prison or even death. It was also crazy to head off on their own into the jungle to chase down one of Billy's stories. And if Ajax could understand, he might never choose to go. But Chuck made the choice for him, because Chuck understood what would happen if they stayed.

It was madness, Chuck knew, but the whole war was madness. And maybe, somehow, through all the madness and death and destruction, they would manage to save this one dog's life. Maybe this was the only sane thing to do after all. Chuck wasn't ready to give up on Ajax. They were breaking out and heading for the border.

CHAPTER 11

OUTSIDE THE WIRE

They gathered again forty minutes later behind the kennel at the perimeter of the base. There were two rows of barbed wire in front of them, with guard towers stretched overhead and listening posts dug into foxholes outside the wire at various points. They wouldn't be safe from detection until they were at least two or three hundred yards away. They had to make that distance while it was still dark.

Billy pulled out wire cutters and went to work on the barbed wire. The guys had their packs on, more filled with rations than with ammunition for this mission, but they were not unarmed.

Chuck and Billy and Double O had their rifles. Billy had two hand grenades and Double O had a grenade and some flares. He'd thought about taking the big machine gun, the sixty-caliber, but the army might chase him down for that. It was worth more to them than he was. So he left it behind.

Doc Malloy had packed extra first-aid supplies and a few colored smoke grenades, but he didn't have a real weapon with him. "We're outnumbered and we're on our own," he explained. "If we get into a firefight with VC, I'll be more useful as a medic than a soldier. And if we get caught by an American patrol, we're not going to shoot at them anyway, right?"

The other three stopped to think about that. They hadn't considered what they'd do if an American patrol tried to stop them. They couldn't attack their own soldiers, but they couldn't just surrender either. That'd be it for Ajax, and they'd all go to jail as deserters for nothing.

"Right," said Chuck at last.

"We better not get caught, then," Double O declared, and they nodded in agreement.

Billy Beans slipped under the barbed wire and then Chuck held it up so Ajax could slide under, followed by Doc Malloy. Double O went last, giving the base a long final look. Billy watched him and couldn't tell if he was happy or sad to be leaving.

They crept along on their bellies, staying as low to the ground as they could. Ajax knew the drill. He crawled along right next to Chuck. For him, there was nothing unusual about their mission, just another night patrol with his best friend and some other guys.

Suddenly, Ajax stopped and perked his ears up. Chuck reached forward and caught Billy's ankle. Billy looked back and saw Chuck and Ajax frozen on the ground. Behind them Doc and Double O had pressed themselves into the earth, their camouflage making them almost invisible in the shadows.

Chuck looked at Ajax, trying to figure out what the alert was about. The army set up their own trip wires around the base. They were attached to flares so that anyone sneaking through the jungle to try to ambush the base would set off a warning signal. Chuck looked around, trying to find a wire, but he couldn't see much in the dark. He tugged at Ajax to see if he could give a better idea what he smelled, but Ajax kept himself planted in place.

The soft brown hairs on his back stood up. He growled and Chuck's blood froze. Ajax wasn't warning them about a trip wire.

Ajax was warning them about a person.

Chuck held his breath. His eyes scanned through the ink-black dark. The darkness that hid them also hid the listening posts around the perimeter of the base. They might stumble right into someone's foxhole if they kept going.

But if they stayed still too long, they'd never make it far enough away by sunrise.

He knew the other three guys were looking to him to make a decision, but he didn't know what to do. He closed his eyes. He pictured himself running through that field with Ajax, safe and dry with nothing but sky above them. No hard choices to make.

"Who's there?" A voice cut the darkness, a terrified whisper. "Who's there?" Again, the voice from the brush.

There was a password they should know. If they had a reason to be out there, they would know the password, and the sentry would know they were friendlies and that they were meant to be in the jungle. But they didn't know the password. It changed every day. They stayed silent, hoping the soldier wouldn't come looking for them.

Chuck opened his eyes and looked in the direction of the voice. He could just make out the shape of a helmet poking up from the ground, ten feet straight ahead of Billy. It was a lone soldier in a foxhole in the dark on the outside of the wire, and he was surely scared out of his wits. A noise in the jungle, a growl. He could think they were the VC about to attack. Or a tiger. Or maybe he thought they were just the wind.

Chuck had spent so many lonely nights in foxholes that he knew the fear the imagination could create all too well. He couldn't let the young guy sit there in agony. And the longer they waited, the more of a chance there was he'd just start firing at them anyway, just to be sure. You never felt safer in a war than when you were squeezing the trigger.

"We're Americans," Chuck whispered back.

He heard Double O exhale behind him. "Shoot, we're cooked now."

"Night patrol," said Chuck. "I forgot the password."

"Chuck?" the voice whispered back. "That you, Chuck?"

Chuck lifted his head. He squinted into the dark and then he crawled forward past Billy, to the foxhole, with Ajax right by his side.

He couldn't see clearly until he was almost on top of it, but the guy in it brushed aside a big, waxy leaf he'd been using to hide the opening and Chuck saw that it was Griffin, standing in muddy water up to his ankles, holding his M16 like a child holds a teddy bear.

"Griff?" Chuck couldn't believe it. "What are you doing out here?"

"I asked for it," said Griffin. "Couldn't stay on base doing nothing, thinking about Bruno. Thinking about you sitting in that kennel. I figured I could clear my head with a night outside the wire standing guard."

"It working?" Chuck asked.

"What do you think?" Griffin grunted. Then he got over the surprise and considered what an odd situation they were in. "What are you doing out here, Chuck? There's no night patrol. And if there was, you wouldn't be on it. They've got you lined up for a Section Eight discharge now, off to the loony bin."

"Guess I lost my chance at the Bronze Star?" Chuck laughed.

Griffin didn't laugh. "You're taking Ajax out?"

Chuck nodded, but Griffin couldn't see him nod in the dark. "Yeah," he answered after the silence dragged on too long.

"You ain't alone, are you?"

Chuck didn't answer. He didn't want to give the guys away, but suddenly Double O was right beside him.

"No," said Double O. "He ain't alone."

This time, Griffin nodded. They couldn't see the expression on his face, just the up-and-down rocking of his head. The silence between them was loaded, deadly as a gun.

Griffin knew that Chuck had Ajax and Double O with him, maybe more guys. He was outnumbered and alone in his foxhole. But they knew that all Griffin had to do was let out a cry to alert the next foxhole down, and in seconds, the whole base would be after them. They'd never get away. They might be shot then and there.

"So, what now?" Chuck asked.

Griffin laughed a sarcastic laugh. He took his helmet off and ran his hand through his bright red hair, and his body shook with laughter. Double O and Billy looked at Chuck nervously. Doc shook his head and whispered something about battlefield hysteria, psychological shock, that kind of thing.

"It ain't that." Griffin pulled himself together, still giggling, but forcing out the words. "It's just funny, you know? It's up to me to choose . . . I went eighteen months in this war without ever having to make a choice harder than picking between eating a can of peaches or a can of chili."

"Everything tastes the same with enough Tabasco on it," said Chuck.

"Right," Griffin said. "No choice at all. But this is the second time today I've been asked to make a real choice. Did you know that, Chuck? With Bruno, just this morning, Morris asked me to choose: Did I want to be there or not?"

Griffin had stopped laughing. In the night, you could see the glint in his eyes. They were wet. Chuck put his hand out, rested it on Griffin's shoulder.

"I stayed with him," said Griffin. "I looked in his eyes. I've been in the war, you know? I mean, real hairy stuff, I've seen. I watched a captain blown to pink powder by a mortar shell the second he stepped off the helicopter into a hot LZ. I watched a private — a seventeen-year-old kid — take a bullet in the nose, right in the nose. He looked so surprised. And that's how he died, with surprise on what was left of his face.

"But I never saw a look like Bruno gave me when I held him there on that table with Morris. His big brown eyes just looked at me, just looked at me for an answer, and he panted a little when Morris put the needle in, but he still looked at me, and I don't know what he was thinking. I wished they could talk, these dogs. I wished it so bad. Then he could have said something, he could've objected or complained or at least, you know, he could've forgiven me. He could've said, 'Hey, pal, it's okay, we had a good time together. We had fun. Don't be too hard on yourself.' But they can't talk, the dogs. They can't forgive us . . ."

"You cared about him," said Chuck. "Nothing to forgive in that."

"I didn't do what you're doing," said Griffin. "I buried two dogs in Vietnam. Two." He sobbed into his helmet, whole body sobs that Chuck could see shaking him, even in the dark.

Ajax shoved his face forward, sliding it along the ground until it was level with Griffin's, and then he didn't need Chuck to give the command — he just let loose with wet dog kisses, licking the salty tears off the weeping soldier's cheeks.

Griffin laughed and gently pushed Ajax back. "Where will you go?" he asked, his voice scratchy with sadness.

"Some Frenchman," said Chuck. "It's a long story."

"I hope so," Griffin answered. "All the stories I've got from this war are short ones."

Chuck squeezed his shoulder.

"Nights so dark like this," said Griffin, "a man can't see a thing." He looked at Chuck and repeated himself. "I can't see a thing."

Chuck nodded.

"There's a trip flare about eight feet in front of you," Griffin added.

"Ajax'll tell us," said Chuck

"Right," said Griffin. "Send me a postcard when you get there."

"I don't think there'll be postcards where we're going. It ain't Paris," whispered Chuck, as he crawled ahead with Ajax at his side. Billy and Double O and Doc followed, each of them nodding their thanks at Griffin as they passed. Griffin didn't look them in the eyes.

They crawled hard through the underbrush until they were far enough away to stand up. Chuck checked his compass and compared it to a map he'd swiped. He knew Laos was the country due west of them. But beyond that, once they were near the border, they'd need more than Billy's cousin's letter to guide them to the Frenchman. If there was a Frenchman to be found, they'd have to ask someone. They'd have to find someone local willing to talk to them.

Chuck didn't know how they'd find someone who would help them, or how they'd communicate without speaking the language. He couldn't believe he'd spent over two years in Vietnam and all he knew how to say in their language was "Hands up!" and "Stop!" He pushed the worries from his mind. He could only take on one impossible task at a time, and right now he was focused on getting them as far from the American base as possible.

Chuck let Ajax do his business on a tree, and then they looked up to the first touches of pink in the sky. It was their first sunrise as deserters from the United States Army. They were criminals now.

Chuck grabbed the chain around his neck and pulled off the small metal dog tags every soldier wore. He looked at the dull metal stamped with his name and serial number. He bent down and dug a small hole in the jungle floor and stuffed his dog tags and their chain into it, then filled it again. The other guys watched him without saying a word. Billy absently rubbed at the spot on his chest where his own dog tags hung, but he didn't move to take them off.

"Too bad I can't take the tattoo off Ajax's ear," said Chuck.

"I'm sure it doesn't bother him," said Doc.

"Bothers me, though," said Chuck. He checked the compass again, nodded once, and pointed the way west. Ajax, as always, took the lead.

CHAPTER 12

LOOKING FOR THE FRENCHMAN

The farther they stayed from the roads and the trails that cut through the countryside, the easier it was to avoid discovery. There would also be fewer booby traps.

But cutting through the brush had its own challenges. It was a harder and a slower way to go. They had to hack vines from their path, cut through razor-sharp elephant grass that jabbed at them through their fatigues, and keep their eyes out for snakes and scorpions. The air was hot and heavy, but the thick brush gave them a kind of safety. It was easy to hide in the jungle.

Suddenly, as they cut through a high hedgerow, hacking away at a tangle of thorny vines, they found themselves staring across an open stretch of rice paddies, a quilt of flooded fields with stalks of rice poking from ankle- and knee-deep

106

water. The morning sun sliced down across the fields, and weary peasant farmers in conical grass hats waded through the water, tending their crops.

The ones nearest the hedge stood up in alarm, staring at the small band of soldiers who had appeared from the jungle without warning. Neither soldiers nor farmers dared to move. Ajax sniffed at the air, his hackles raised, his tail rigid.

"Yeah," whispered Chuck. "I could have used a warning *before* we cut through the hedge into the middle of these people's farmland."

"What do we do now?" whispered Billy.

"We keep going," said Double O. "Longer we stand here, the more time word has to spread that there are Americans walking through the area. We don't need anybody knowing we're here. Let's go."

Double O waved at the farmers, flashing a toothy grin, and stepped past Chuck and Ajax into the rice paddy. His boots made a sucking sound with each step, but he walked forward confidently, holding his gun at the ready just in case. A raised red dirt path cut through the wet fields about one hundred yards to their east, where a boy on a blue bicycle rode by. He turned his head when he saw the Americans with their big dog, and he followed them with his eyes even as his bike kept going forward. He rode right off the path and into the water with a splash.

Billy laughed and Ajax barked at the sudden noise. Several of the farmers ducked and covered their heads.

The boy climbed out of the water and hauled his bike up onto the path again. He hopped on and pumped his legs furiously, racing for the small village in the distance.

"They must have run into American patrols before," noted Doc Malloy. "Otherwise, why would they be so nervous?"

"I guess that boy'll have a story to tell when he gets home," said Billy.

"Well, we should be worried about who he tells his story to," said Double O. "Could be VC in that village."

"Keep your rifles on safety," said Chuck. "But stay alert. VC loves to hide traps in rice paddies." He moved in front of Double O so that Ajax could sniff out any threats better. The smell of the fields was strong — stale water and an earthy animal stench. Chuck worried Ajax wouldn't be able to smell hidden explosives through it. But they didn't have time to slow down. The boy was almost back at the village in the distance. Word of the Americans was going to spread fast.

"Better pick up the pace," said Chuck. He urged Ajax forward faster. The water in the flooded rice paddies came halfway up Ajax's belly, and the dog had to do an odd sort of bounding leap to make any progress. The mud pulled on his paws, and some of his steps were uncertain. He vanished under the surface every few yards so that Chuck had to haul him back out, soaked. Ajax sneezed and shook the filthy water off his fur. He gave Chuck a look of dismay.

"Don't worry buddy," Chuck told the dog. "Not too much farther." When he looked up after forty minutes, though, it seemed like they still had a long way to go before they reached the jungle-covered mountains again. They'd be safer when they got there.

As they walked through the marshy farmland, they were totally exposed to view from all sides, the four AWOL soldiers and their stolen dog. They could be seen from all the fields and from the raised dirt paths that crisscrossed among them, from the far mountains they were walking toward, and from the small village they had to walk past to get there. The farmers watched them nervously. No one spoke to them.

"I hope they don't know we're on our own out here," said Billy.

"Just walk with confidence," said Doc. "They'll assume we're part of a larger unit. Let's do nothing to make them think otherwise."

The high grass along the edge of the fields made Doc nervous. An entire enemy battalion could be hiding in that grass, and they wouldn't know it until too late. An entire American battalion could be hiding there too. Doc wasn't sure which was worse — to be shot by the enemy because they were Americans, or to be shot by the Americans because they were deserters.

After a few minutes pushing through a deep field, Ajax stopped. Billy didn't notice. He kept going, taking a few steps ahead of Chuck.

"Come on, Ajax," Chuck pulled the leash. "We've got to keep going." Ajax pressed himself lower in the water, his jaw resting just above the scummy surface. Chuck cocked his head at him, studied the hairs on his back, the point of his ears and tail. He raised his arm and the other guys stopped. "Don't move!" he called. "Ajax alerted to something."

"What? What is it? A trap?" Billy's eyes got wide. He saw he was in front, ahead of the scout dog, and he cursed himself for having taken the lead. He remembered Chuck's warning about traps hidden in the rice paddies, and it made his skin tingle.

He scanned the water around his knees. Tiny bubbles broke the surface, but the water was too murky to see through. Could he have stepped on a trip wire somewhere down below? Could he be on a booby trap right now, caught in that time before it went off, still alive, but beyond help? Was this how he'd die? He swallowed hard. He closed his eyes and whispered a prayer.

"Yea, though I walk through the valley," he said.

"Chill out," said Double O.

Billy opened his eyes and desperately looked back at Chuck and Ajax.

"If it were a booby trap, you'd be dead already," said Chuck. "It's something else."

Chuck looked at his dog and then looked around. The sun had vanished. The sky was a pale green soup. The rain was holding off, but it wouldn't for long. The earth was red, the rice paddies a mix of greens and browns, like a sloppy finger-painting done by a child who couldn't draw people.

Chuck's heart skipped a beat.

There were no people.

The farmers had gone, vanished, nowhere in sight. He hadn't seen them go. The wind waved through the tall grass. Time unstitched itself again, moving too slow, moving too fast. Something was about to happen. You didn't need a dog's powerful senses to feel it.

"Where are all the people?" Double O spoke Chuck's worry out loud.

Billy flipped the safety off on his rifle and rested his finger over the trigger. So did Double O. So did Chuck.

There was no real cover. They were still at least three hundred yards from the jungle on the mountains and they were maybe one hundred yards from the quiet village.

Ajax whimpered.

"What does he — ?" Billy started, but Chuck held his hand up for silence, and his face strained with listening. And then Chuck heard what Ajax had heard.

Helicopters.

The other guys heard it too. They all looked up.

The unmistakable drumming of American helicopters beating their way across the sky.

"They looking for us?" Billy asked, shifting on his feet, making squishing sounds in the mud below the water.

"Not a chance," said Doc. "They wouldn't send choppers out for some deserters. Probably just routine flights. Moving soldiers here or there. Moving supplies. Anything, really."

"If they see us, we're done. They'll call it in," said Chuck.

"Are they coming this way?"

"One sound I know for sure is the sound of a helicopter coming my way," said Chuck.

"How long do we have?" asked Doc.

"Not long enough to make it to cover," said Chuck.

The thumping of the helicopter blades grew louder.

"Everyone down!" Chuck commanded, and they all dove for the edge of the rice paddy and slid low into the dirty water. Chuck pulled Ajax on his lap and held him tightly, keeping the dog's head above water, but keeping him still.

The helicopters appeared over the treetops, blades beating the air, engines roaring. There were two of them, flying low over the trees.

"Stay perfectly still," whispered Double O, who had his eyes and nose just above the water line, peering up. He could see the barrels of the big machine guns poking from the open sides of the helicopters. He knew that the door gunners were itching to rain fire on anything that moved below.

If the helicopters thought they were VC and opened fire, there would be nothing they could do about it. They'd be torn apart by bullets, killed by their own side, and they'd sink into the dirty water and maybe never be heard of again. Double O shivered. This was how the farmers must feel every time the American choppers flew over their fields and their villages: helpless. And afraid.

The helicopters buzzed above, circling the village, making ripples in the shallow water, but they must not have found what they were looking for, because after about ten minutes they flew off again, continuing on their way and disappearing over the treetops. Double O exhaled, but no one moved until long after the sound of the helicopters had faded.

"We have to get out of the open," said Chuck. He let go of Ajax and stood. The dog scampered up on the red, dirty path above the rice paddies and shook himself off, splattering mud and stinking water all over the soldiers. Only Chuck had managed to turn his face away in time. The rest of them found themselves spitting and wiping muck from their eyes.

"Leeches," said Doc, reaching over to pull one of the thin, black, bloodsucking slugs from Billy's neck.

"Ow!" said Billy.

"Check yourselves for leeches," warned Doc.

"No time," said Chuck. "We'll do it when we've got some cover."

"To the mountains?" Billy asked.

"No," said Chuck. "The village."

The others looked at him like he was crazy.

"If there's an old Frenchman's plantation on the other side of those mountains, the villagers might know something about it," he said.

"How we gonna ask 'em?" said Double O. "Billy barely speaks English, so I don't think he's got any Vietnamese, and I sure know I don't speak a word of it."

"And, Chuck," added Doc. "Even if we can figure out how to ask them a question, they didn't seem too eager to get to know us. They hid the second they heard those helicopters coming."

"We've got to try," said Chuck. "It's the only way we're going to find this Frenchman's mansion."

The others looked at him doubtfully.

"Come on," said Chuck, thinking of the nobleman in the old paperback he'd been reading. "It's quixotic, remember?"

Doc shook his head. "Don Quixote is about a man *pretending* to be a knight. He's not a knight, though. He's crazy."

"Crazy," said Chuck. "But noble too. People help him on his quest; people *want* to help him."

"Does the book have a happy ending?" asked Billy. "Because I don't think our story will if we walk into that village like pretend knights on a crazy quest."

Chuck shrugged. "I never finished the book."

"Quixotic isn't a good thing," said Doc. "To be like Don Quixote is to be a dreamer. Unrealistic."

"Sounds like a good thing to me," said Billy.

"We've got enough *realistic* in this war to last a lifetime," Double O agreed. "Maybe it's time we give *quixotic* a chance."

Doc sighed and gave in. It was three against one, after all, and Chuck was right: They didn't have much of a choice.

Chuck waved them forward and stepped out ahead with Ajax, heading toward the village. He wished he'd finished reading that old book. He could really use a happy ending right about now.

CHAPTER 13

THE SOLDIERS IN THE SCHOOLHOUSE

The village wasn't much to look at. High hedges ringed it on three sides, and only the moldering ruins of an old Buddhist temple could be seen poking over the top. Its spire was crumbling, its statues long gone.

The tangle of hedges opened into a central clearing with a long, low concrete building at the far end. It had a front porch with high columns. Other buildings with tin roofs were scattered around the big building, and narrow paths cut between them. The smallest buildings had thatched roofs; they were more like huts, made from the same mud that was caked on the soldiers' pants and that was packed into the roads. The muddy ground was puddled with footprints, but Chuck and the others couldn't see any of the people who had made them.

"They're here," said Double O as they fanned out in a line and walked across the clearing. They held their weapons low but ready. "They're just hiding."

Ajax was on high alert, walking close to Chuck's side, his nose twitching in the air, pulling in all the village smells — wood smoke from cooking fires, rotting garbage and decay, human waste and sweat. It was a poor village, but it smelled lived-in.

"It's creepy," said Billy, "knowing we're being watched."

"Well, Sir Knight," said Doc. "What now?"

"Hello!" Chuck called out. "Anybody? We need some help!"

The dark doorways stayed dark. The village answered with silence.

"I guess they never read that book of yours," said Billy.

Chuck looked down at Ajax. The hair on his back was sticking up. His tail was pointed. He was signaling that there were people there. His low growl told Chuck there were a lot of them. Why wouldn't they show themselves?

The Americans were there to help, after all. They were supposed to be the good guys in this part of the country. Of course, the VC had friendly villages all over the south of Vietnam. It was hard to tell who was a good guy and who was a bad guy, when they all dressed the same and spoke the same language and lived in the same villages.

"I can't believe I'm doing this," said Double O, stopping and letting out a long sigh. He bent down and set his gun carefully on the ground, then stood again and raised his hands in the air, palms open. "We come in peace!" he yelled.

Doc nodded. He didn't have a gun to put down, but he held his hands up high too, to show he meant no harm. Chuck looked at Billy, who shook his head slightly, his eyes wide.

"No way," he mouthed.

Chuck nodded slowly and set his own rifle down on the ground. "Sit," he commanded, and Ajax sat. "Lie down," he said. Ajax looked up at him, puzzled. "Lie down," Chuck repeated.

Ajax groaned, but he settled down into the mud, fighting all his instincts to hop up and bark and snarl.

"Good boy," Chuck said.

"I changed my mind," said Billy. "This *is* crazy. This could be a VC village. Communist sympathizers. Heck, we don't even know where we are. This could be North Vietnam. Enemy territory. I'm not dropping my gun."

"Have some faith, Billy," said Double O, although the waver in his voice sounded like he was trying to give himself the same advice. "We're being quixotic."

"Quixotic. Right," said Billy. "If you're wrong about this, I'm never trusting a novel ever again." He put his rifle on the ground and raised his hands high. "I hope they don't think we're surrendering to them."

"Now why would they think that?" said Doc, holding his hands higher over his head. Billy couldn't believe Doc was being sarcastic at a time like this, but he appreciated the humor.

In a flash, Ajax sprang to his feet and started barking. Chuck grabbed him and held him back, but looked up to see what had set him off.

A boy, maybe ten or eleven years old, peeked out from behind one of the columns in front of the long, low building. He had pressed himself behind it when Ajax barked, but they could still see his arm and the edge of his red T-shirt.

"That's the kid from before, with the bike," said Double O.

"How do you know?" asked Billy.

"I'm Double O, man," said Double O. "Superspy."

"And his bike is leaning against the other column," said Doc, gesturing with his chin but keeping his hands high.

"It's okay," Chuck called out to the boy, taking slow steps toward the column and keeping Ajax, growling lowly, tight at his side. "He won't hurt you."

"Kid doesn't understand you," said Double O. "But Ajax is speaking the universal language."

"It's okay," Chuck said again, raising his voice to higher pitch, speaking as gently as he could. "Can you help us? Help?"

Chuck squatted down so that the boy was above him on the small porch. He petted Ajax to calm him. "It's okay," Chuck repeated, over and over, like a prayer. "It's okay. It's okay. It's okay." He didn't really know what else to say.

The boy peered around the column, his eyes dark and wide. Fear and curiosity wrestled across his face, but curiosity won, and he stepped toward Chuck. Ajax grumbled, but Chuck shushed him. He mimed holding his hand out, hoping the boy would understand. He did.

The boy put his hand out and Chuck let Ajax sniff it, still holding the dog tight, just in case. Ajax, smelling no threat, seemed to relax as his nose worked over the boy's hand. His tail started to wag, splattering mud into the air behind him.

"Ajax," Chuck whispered. "Kiss."

Ajax stood and immediately doused the boy's face with his tongue. The boy cringed at first, stepping backward, but the tongue tickled his face and he laughed. He let Ajax keep licking him, and though he wrinkled his nose at the dog's breath, he laughed hysterically now. Ajax snuffled at the boy's shirt and poked him with his snout, eager to play.

Chuck smiled. The boy smiled back.

"I knew *kiss* would come in handy," Chuck told the guys.

The boy started petting Ajax, running his hand over the dog's head, smoothing his ears back and letting them pop up again as he ran his tiny palm down the dog's broad brown-and-black back. Ajax was loving it. He flopped down into the mud freely and rolled over, showing his belly, demanding belly rubs.

"He likes you," Chuck told the boy. The boy smiled and imitated Chuck, rubbing Ajax's belly, even though he surely couldn't understand a word the big American soldier was saying. Unlike humans, dogs knew how to make themselves understood without words. Ajax was teaching them both how to talk to each other.

Chuck started to feel hopeful. He rummaged in his pack and pulled out Ajax's favorite toy, the old rope with the can. He raised his arm to toss it.

"No!" shouted a woman in a black shirt, rushing from inside the largest building, her sandals slapping at the mud as she ran. "No VC here!" she yelled. "You go! You go! No VC!"

Ajax barked as the woman ran forward and the boy yelped, leaping away, his joy turning instantly to terror. Chuck grabbed Ajax and pulled him back as the woman reached the boy and grabbed him by the shirt collar in the same way, yanking him to her side and stepping in front of him, placing her body between the boy and the dog.

"You go," she said. "You no stay here."

"It's okay." Chuck stood and held his palm up, his other hand keeping Ajax back. The dog was still barking and snarling at the woman, his fangs bared and his eyes flashing fury. Behind Chuck, Billy and Double O took tiny steps back, moving toward their guns on the ground, just in case. The Vietcong had many female soldiers and spies, and you could never tell if one of them was disguised as a civilian.

"I'd feel a whole lot better with my gun," whispered Billy.

"For once, we agree," Double O whispered back.

"We mean no harm," said Chuck. "Quiet, Ajax!"

Ajax quieted. Chuck ordered him to sit, and Ajax obeyed, but his eyes stayed fixed on the angry woman.

"Peace," said Chuck. He raised two fingers, flashing her the peace sign. "We come in peace, understand?"

"I speak English," the woman said. Her accent was thick, but her words were clear. "I am the teacher here. You must go. Go now. Leave here."

The woman was afraid. Chuck wondered of what. Was she afraid the Americans were going to start shooting up the village, or was she afraid the Vietcong would attack if they knew Americans were in the village? Did she not like dogs or did she not like soldiers? If Chuck were in her position, wouldn't he be afraid too?

"We will leave," said Chuck. "But first, we need help."

As she looked Chuck up and down, the boy peeked out from behind the woman's legs. He whispered something to her, and she shushed him in a way that Chuck recognized from his own school days. It hadn't been that long since he was a schoolboy himself, really, but it felt like a lifetime ago.

"Please help us, mama-san," he said. Her brow furrowed, and he worried that he'd offended her. "I mean, uh, ma'am," he said. "Please."

The woman pressed her hands together as she thought. The boy clung to her leg. Her eyes flickered back to the other three soldiers.

"We have a medic with us." Chuck pointed to Doc. "If you have any injured or sick in your village, perhaps he can help?"

"Medic?" she said. "Like a doctor?"

"Yes," said Chuck. "Like a doctor."

The woman's expression softened. She nodded. "Come inside here," she said. "Quick, quick." She looked around at the other buildings and sighed. "Leave your weapons."

"Yes, ma'am," said Chuck, and he signaled for the guys to follow.

As they stepped to the dark opening of the doorway, the woman stopped and turned to Chuck. "No dog," she said. "He stay outside."

"I'm sorry, ma'am," Chuck answered. "Ajax has to come with me."

"No," she said firmly. "No dog inside. Never." She looked Chuck square in the eye. Her small body seemed to fill the whole doorway, unmoving.

Chuck blew out through his cheeks and nodded. He tied Ajax up to the column in front of the door. "You stay here, pal," he whispered to his dog. "We'll be right inside, okay? You be a good boy." He rubbed the dog's head and went inside. Ajax whimpered as Chuck left, but the boy rushed from the woman's side and ran to Ajax again.

"Keess!" the boy shouted. "Keess! Keess!"

Ajax cocked his head at the boy. The woman looked back with alarm, but Chuck saw Ajax's tail wagging and he smiled.

"Smart kid," he said, and whistled from the doorway.

Ajax looked at him.

"Kiss!" Chuck called and Ajax obeyed, stretching to the end of the leash and slobbering all over the boy again. The kid squealed with delight and grabbed the dog's toy, setting off a tugging match that he was sure to lose. The boy and the dog grunted and rolled in the mud as they played. It was unclear who was enjoying it more — or who was getting dirtier in the process.

Once she saw that the boy would be okay, the woman led Chuck through the doorway, followed by Billy, Double O, and Doc.

"We have many sick people," said the woman. "You will help?"

"I'll do what I can," said Doc.

Chuck looked around the dim space. It was filled with frightened faces, young and old, men and women, watching the soldiers' every move. Benches had been pushed around the room to act as beds. Along the far wall was a cracked blackboard with chalky ghosts smudged across it.

"A schoolhouse," he said.

"It was," the woman answered.

Chuck wondered if there were people gathered like this in all the buildings, hiding and watching, waiting for the Americans to leave their village. Waiting for the war to end. Chuck wondered where all the other schoolchildren were.

The woman spoke to the room in Vietnamese, giving some sort of speech. As she talked, she pointed at the American soldiers. Some people nodded, others coughed. A few clicked their tongues against their teeth or asked questions.

When the woman was done, the crowd parted in the middle, and she gestured for Doc to go to a young man lying on a bench along the back wall. Even in the dim light, it was obvious that he was not well.

His arm hung limp off to the side, almost touching the floor. His skin had almost no color, and his eyes stared vacantly at the ceiling. The only true sign of life in him was the sound of a low whistle as he struggled to breathe. The man sitting next to him held a damp cloth pressed to the young man's forehead.

As Doc approached, the other man lifted the sick man's shirt and Doc stopped. He stared at the wound and then looked up at the crowd in the room. His heartbeat quickened.

The young man wasn't simply sick. He had a wound in his stomach, and it was swollen and oozing with infection.

"An accident," explained the woman, but Doc looked back at Chuck with eyebrows raised, trying to signal something else. He rolled his eyes around at the crowd, trying to tell Chuck to look closely at the people in the room, at the large number of young men watching them closely, watching them nervously, but Chuck couldn't read Doc's expressions the way he could read Ajax's, so he just nodded encouragement for Doc to tend to the young man's wound.

Only Doc knew the wound was no accident. He had seen too many wounds just like it on other young men.

It was a gunshot wound.

CHAPTER 14

IN ENEMY HANDS

The way Doc figured it, at least half the people in the schoolhouse with them were enemy soldiers, pretending to be civilians. It was the only explanation for why there would be so many young men when they had never seen any in a village before. And it would explain the gunshot wound and why the woman was lying about it.

Doc wished they hadn't left all their weapons lying in the dirt. He wished Ajax were inside with Chuck instead of tied up outside playing with a kid. He felt helpless, but until he could warn the others, he had to do whatever he could for the wounded man in front of him.

He knelt down and felt the man's fever with the back of his hand and started rummaging in his pack to find something to ease the man's pain. There wasn't much else he could do to help the guy, but it would at least make him look busy, and buy them some time. He started to wonder if American soldiers had shot this man, maybe even if his own unit had shot him in their firefight last week.

While Doc worked, Chuck turned to the woman. "Can you help us as well?" he asked.

The woman nodded.

"We're looking for a Frenchman," he said. Billy brought over the letter from his cousin that described the Frenchman's mansion with its chandelier and its fine china plates and marble floors. And its dogs. The woman read the letter carefully.

"There are many words here I do not know," she said. She pointed at a few. Chuck looked at Billy and shook his head. They were all curse words and a few dirty words about a certain famous actress.

"What?" said Billy. "My cousin's a marine, not a member of the good manners club."

"They got a club for that?" Double O joked.

"Don't worry about those words," Chuck explained. "What about the place? Do you know a place like he describes?"

The woman thought. She called out some questions in Vietnamese and some of the men in the room answered. One of them laughed. The woman snapped at him and a brief argument started among the men, but she ended it simply by raising her hand in the air.

"I guess teachers have a lot more power here than they do back home," said Billy.

"Nah," said Double O. "My mom can do that too. Teachers gotta have attitude. It's true all over the world. No such thing as a weak teacher, least not for long."

The woman smiled politely and then spoke to Chuck. "Why do you want to find this place? Is this your mission?"

Chuck looked at the others. He could lie and say yes, and make this woman think the full force of the United States Army demanded her cooperation, or he could be honest and tell her the truth, that they were on their own, fleeing their own countrymen just to save a good dog's life.

Outside, he heard Ajax barking playfully and the boy laughing. He turned back to the woman.

"It's my dog, ma'am," he said, and then he told her the story. She listened carefully, but her expression showed no change as he told her about Ajax's bravery and skill and how the army planned to put him down, and about how they'd abandoned their duty as soldiers to save him.

When he was done, she turned to the room and started repeating the story to them in their language. He couldn't tell if she was arguing for or against helping him. The men had a lot of opinions, which they expressed loudly.

"There may be such a place," the woman told Chuck.

Relief washed over him. He pulled out his map and handed it to her. "Can you show me?"

The woman carried it to a group of young men, who immediately began pointing at it and arguing, jabbing their fingers at different places and waving their fingers in each other's faces.

"Nothing's ever simple, is it?" Double O asked no one in particular.

Doc left the injured man's side and stepped over to Chuck and the others.

"Guys," he whispered. "We have to get out of here."

"What? Why?" said Billy.

"You notice anything strange about this place?"

"The whole country's strange to me," said Billy.

"The men," whispered Doc. "Look at the men."

Double O glanced around. He was the first to get what Doc was saying. Most of the women were holding their children close and trying not to look at the Americans. They were afraid. But the men — the men were not afraid. They had a look Double O knew well, a look he'd seen all his life, from guards in department stores and doormen at fancy apartment buildings and from cops. It was a look that said loud and clear, "You're not welcome here."

"He's right," said Double O. "We should get out of here."

"They're helping us," Chuck said.

"Or they're just waiting to take us prisoner," said Double O.

"This is a VC village. I'm sure of it," said Doc.

Double O agreed. "Wish I'd seen it sooner. Never should have come here. Never should have put our guns down."

"It was your idea to put the guns down!" hissed Billy.

"Just 'cause it was my idea doesn't make it a good one," Double O snapped back at him.

"I think it may have been unwise to tell them the truth," said Doc. "Did you know there's a cash reward for anyone who brings the Vietcong commandos the tattooed ear of a United States Military scout dog?"

"Yeah," sighed Chuck. "I know."

"So even if these people are not VC, they are now in a position to earn money by helping the VC and hurting us. And this village looks like it could use some money."

From the bench, the wounded man groaned. The woman left the men with the map and came over to Doc Malloy.

"Can you help him?" she asked. The men looked up from the map and watched him closely.

"I gave him some medicine for the pain," said Doc. "But the wound is bad. If he can't get to a real hospital, he will die. There is nothing I can do here to treat an infected gunshot wound."

The woman nodded, understanding.

"He is not a bad man," she said. "My cousin."

Doc didn't say anything. Sometimes, silence was the only appropriate answer. Outside, the boy laughed with Ajax.

"I think we should leave your village before dark," Chuck said.

"He is like you," the woman said. She looked at him. "He left his army. All these men." She gestured to the men with the map, about a dozen of them. "They were with the Vietcong, yes. I know you know this."

Chuck heard Double O clear his throat but he kept eye contact with the woman, letting her tell her story, as she had let him tell his.

"They fought to protect their homes from invaders — first the French, then the Americans," she said. "I do not apologize for this. In war, no side is all right or all wrong. We want freedom and we want peace. My cousin is young and he believed these things could be gained with guns. So he fought, all these men fought. Last week, they captured a unit of soldiers from the ARVN, our own people, fighting with the Americans. Their officer ordered them to shoot the prisoners. All of them."

She shook her head, sadly. "In war there is death, yes. But this, to kill prisoners. It was murder. My cousin refused. He wanted to fight for his country, not murder his countrymen. The officer was angry. The officer yelled. The officer threatened him if he did not shoot the prisoners. Still, he refused."

Chuck could picture it: the frightened prisoner, the frightened soldiers holding him prisoner, the impossible choice. What a monstrous thing war was, he thought. The choices they all had to make: loyalty to their side or doing the right thing. Most of the time, it was hard to know what the right thing was.

"These men" — the woman gestured at the other young men in the room — "they stood with my cousin; they would not shoot the prisoners either. They know what is right. The officer pointed his gun at my cousin, accused him of treason. The men pointed their guns at the officer. And someone fired."

Chuck shuddered. If they had been caught fleeing with Ajax, would the same scene have unfolded? Would it be Billy or Double O lying on a bench somewhere, disowned by his country?

"The officer was shot, dead. My cousin was shot too," said the woman. "The prisoners escaped, and these men fled. They carried my cousin here only yesterday. And now you have come here too, running. We are a village now for those who are running away."

"We aren't running away," Billy corrected her. "We're running *to* somewhere. There's a difference."

"Yes," said the woman. "But, like my cousin, you have left your army for what you think is right."

"It *is* right," said Chuck, more certain than ever.

"Yes." The woman nodded, but it wasn't clear if she was agreeing, or simply ending the conversation. She went back to the men, presumably giving them the bad news about her cousin. Then she took the map from them and they pointed to it and talked some more.

"See?" said Chuck. "They're helping."

"But they're VC," said Billy. "The enemy. Just because they deserted their side, doesn't make them not VC. I mean, we're still American, right?"

"So what?" said Chuck. "VC, Charlie, ARVN, communist, socialist, US Army, who cares? They're all just names for the same thing. Just people. And right now, we're just people trying to do a good thing for a dog who needs it. We're not here to fight them. We're here for Ajax."

"Yeah," said Billy. "Because Ajax saved us from *people* just like them who were trying to kill us."

"We were trying to kill them too," said Chuck. "It's war. The only one innocent in all this is Ajax."

"They cannot be certain," the woman said, returning with the map. "But the place you are seeking may be here." She jabbed her finger at a point on the map, about another full day's hike away. "There is much fighting in the hills along the way. You must be careful."

"We'll do our best," said Chuck. "Thank you." He folded the map and put it in his pocket. He nodded his thanks to the men sitting along the wall, knowing they had been, until recently, his enemy.

"If you would like to eat with us," said the woman, "you are welcome to stay longer. We do not have much, but what we have, we will share."

"No, thank you," Chuck told her. "You've done more than enough. I'm sorry we couldn't do more for you."

She joined her palms together and bowed her head. Then she turned to sit beside her cousin and hold his hand as his breathing slowed and his heartbeat faded.

Chuck stepped outside. Billy and Double O rushed across the courtyard to pick up their weapons, which remained exactly where they had been left.

Doc Malloy stood next to Chuck and looked down at Ajax and the boy. They had both worn themselves out playing. Ajax was still tied around the pillar, but he'd curled up beside it to sleep. The boy slept too, curled up with Ajax, using the big dog as a pillow. One of Ajax's paws rested across the boy's chest, like a hug.

"I guess there are two innocents in all this," said Doc.

"But we can only save one of them," Chuck said. "Let's move out."

He stepped over to Ajax and squatted down to untie him. The dog sighed as he woke up and stretched out all four of his legs. As he stretched, the boy awoke with a yawn. He looked up at Chuck and smirked. Chuck smirked back at him.

"Sorry, little guy. Playtime's over," he told the kid, who he knew couldn't understand a word he said. Ajax stood and nudged the boy with his nose, knocking him sideways. "Playtime's over for you too, Ajax." Chuck laughed and pulled the dog away from his new friend.

Ajax whined.

"I think your dog likes our village very much," the woman said, standing in the doorway. Her cheeks were puffy and her eyes damp, like she had just been crying.

"I guess so," said Chuck. Chuck looked over his shoulder to Billy and Double O, wiping down their rifles, and Doc Malloy, reorganizing his medical kit. "I suppose we can let them play for a few more minutes."

He looked down at Ajax. The dog looked back up at him, his tail wagging. As soon as their eyes met, Ajax sat and perked his ears. It was his way of asking for something, showing off what a good dog he could be.

"How can I say no to that face?" Chuck shook his head and let go of the leash. Ajax immediately bounded over to the boy again, knocking him down with a friendly whack of his paw, and in an instant the boy and the dog were rolling together in the mud, giggling and barking.

Chuck was amazed at how gentle Ajax could be. His mind flashed back to the image of his dog pulling that VC prisoner from the tunnel, a guy who could have been fighting with the men of this very village, and here was Ajax, at peace and at play just a few days later. It gave him hope. The world wasn't such an ugly place after all, as long as a boy and a dog could play.

The other guys came over and stood beside Chuck, watching the wrestling match. Double O shook his head in disbelief, wondering why anyone would want to roll in the mud with a dog like that. Billy thought about his own dogs back home, how much he hoped he'd get to see them again. Doc's thoughts were still back in the dim building, wondering if he'd done all he could for the wounded man, doubting himself.

Suddenly, Ajax stopped playing. He stood up straight and perked his ears. The boy still had his arm wrapped around Ajax's neck and the dog lifted him right off the ground as he stood. Then Ajax growled, and the boy fell. He scurried backward on hands and feet like a crab.

"Don't worry." Chuck rushed for Ajax. He grabbed the leash as he explained to the woman. "He's not attacking. He's warning us."

"About what?" said Billy.

"Shh," Chuck snapped. "Someone's coming."

"More choppers?" asked Billy.

"I don't hear choppers," said Double O.

"Shh!" Chuck snapped again. "Listen."

They stood silently in the muddy village square, listening, the soldiers, the dog, the boy, and the teacher.

"Trucks," said the woman. "I hear trucks."

They all heard it, the groan of truck engines pushing their way through the mud, heading toward the village.

"Americans?" asked Billy.

"I don't think so," said Doc.

Double O was the first to see the puff of black smoke from a struggling diesel engine rising from the trees. Then they all saw a jeep followed by a covered personnel carrier emerge from a narrow jungle road, bouncing along the muddy road that led through the rice paddies to the village.

"ARVN," said Double O. "South Vietnamese Army."

"At least they're on our side," said Billy.

"But they're not on the side of those guys in that building," said Chuck.

The soldiers looked at each other, none of them knowing what to do. The woman ran back into the building to warn the others.

"We gotta get out of here," said Double O. "Whatever happens, it's none of our concern. This is a problem between the Vietnamese. And we don't want to be around when it goes down."

"No time to get to the jungle," said Chuck. "We've got to hide and wait it out."

The men agreed. They looked back at the schoolhouse, which had gone as dark and quiet as when they'd first arrived in the village, and then they rushed out to take cover in one of the rice paddies.

As they left, Chuck glanced back and saw the boy's face in the dark opening of the building. He was waving at Ajax. Then the woman pulled him away, and the village fell as silent as a grave.

CHAPTER 15

TAKING SIDES

The South Vietnamese soldiers of the ARVN rolled into the village with a thunder of activity. A commander jumped from the jeep, holding a pistol. He started shouting as soon as his feet touched the ground, and soldiers poured from the back of the truck, their rifles in their arms. They scurried around, taking up positions in the courtyard.

Crouched down again in the muck of a flooded rice paddy, Chuck held Ajax low and stroked his ears to keep him quiet. Billy gripped his rifle close to his chest and closed his eyes, listening, while Doc sat next to him, looking up at the sky and trying to ignore the thought that, below the water, a horde of black leeches was surely sliming its way into his boots and up his pants legs to prey on his soft, pink skin.

Double O peeked over the top of the paddy, gazing through the tall elephant grass as the soldiers overran the village. He thought back to spying on Chuck and Doc, preparing to run their ridiculous covert operation to seize the ping-pong table. At least Chuck and Ajax were on his side this time. He couldn't believe that had happened only a week ago.

"What's going on?" whispered Billy, who didn't dare raise his head to look for himself.

"That teacher's come out to talk to the commander," Double O said, watching the woman, alone in the courtyard, speaking to the commander with her hands folded in front of her, looking down at her feet. She looked so small and weak, nothing like the fierce woman who could silence a room of men by raising her arm in the air. She was putting on a show for the soldiers.

Double O watched as the commander nodded like he was listening carefully, then pointed his pistol right at the woman. She gasped. The little boy came running from inside the building and clutched at the woman's side.

"That boy must be her son," said Double O.

The commander seemed to soften when he saw the boy. The men behind him shifted nervously with their rifles.

The commander spoke to the boy; he crouched down to the boy's level and asked him questions. The boy shook his head in big side-to-side motions. Even from far away Double O could tell the boy was answering whatever had been asked with a lie. Little boys are rarely very good liars. The commander stood and rubbed the boy's hair as he talked again to his mother.

Then he raised his pistol, putting it gently against the boy's head, right in the spot where he'd just ruffled his hair.

The boy froze.

The woman dropped to her knees, pleading.

"Just give them up," Double O whispered, willing the woman to give in, to protect her son. The woman wasn't giving up, though.

The commander barked an order at his men and a small group stormed into the big building. Double O cringed, waiting to hear gunshots, the eruption of a firefight, but no shots came.

There was some shouting, and then a silence as heavy as Double O had ever heard, and then, one by one, the Vietcong from inside the building stepped outside with their hands up, prisoners of the young soldiers of the ARVN, their fellow countrymen.

How could they do this to their own?

Double O thought back to those images he'd seen on the news, of cops beating up protesters in Selma, Alabama; cops beating up protesters in Chicago; protesters turning into angry mobs in Watts and Detroit and the Bronx. Americans, all. He'd said it before, and now he realized how true it was: The Vietnamese and the Americans weren't all that different. Both were capable of heroism, and both could just as easily become monsters.

The woman's face crumpled as she watched the men being led out of the building and loaded onto the truck. Even her cousin's now lifeless body was carried out and tossed like a sack of rice into the back.

The woman wept and pleaded with the commander, but he ignored her, keeping his gun steady as he shouted at his men. The engine of their jeep roared to life. The truck sputtered and idled. The women and children from inside the building huddled in the doorway, watching with blank faces. They did not look afraid. They looked, simply, exhausted.

The commander finally lowered his gun from the boy's head, gave him a chillingly friendly smile, and walked back to the truck. The boy stood still as a statue.

The woman crawled after the commander on her knees through the mud, covering her clothes in filth, begging. Double O guessed she wanted her cousin's body back. The commander continued to ignore her. She grabbed his pants leg, just as her boy had grabbed her pants leg when Ajax had barked at him.

The commander stopped.

He turned to the woman, and without hesitation, he slapped her across the face. She fell backward, and he stepped over her, walking briskly back to her son with his gun raised. The boy took two hesitant steps back as the commander pressed the gun to his head once more. He cocked the hammer of the pistol back, ready to fire. The woman screamed.

Double O felt something bump him to the side in the grass. He looked down and saw Ajax shoot like a rocket onto the mud path, racing to the village square, barking furiously. Chuck scrambled after him, trying to call him back without shouting. The commander turned to look at Ajax, an expression of confusion on his face, and then he pointed his gun away from the boy and at the dog.

"No!" Chuck yelled, but his own rifle was still hanging from his shoulder.

Before the commander could fire, before Double O even knew what he was doing, he'd pressed his rifle to his shoulder and aimed down the barrel at the commander's chest.

The commander lifted his pistol higher, taking aim at the charging dog. Ajax leapt from the ground, launching himself like a missile at the commander, whose finger tensed on the trigger of his gun.

And then Double O stood tall in the grass with his rifle hot in his hands and he squeezed the trigger.

CHAPTER 16

THE WARRIOR'S CODE

The burst of gunfire seemed to slow down time.

The commander fell backward into the mud, his pistol still in his hand, his head bent at an impossible angle. Ajax landed in the mud beside him and sniffed curiously. Then he trotted over to the boy and licked his face.

No one else moved. It was like time had frozen for everyone but the dog.

Even Double O himself stood still, his gun barrel smoking. His eyebrows were lifted in surprise, like he hadn't really expected to shoot.

The commander was dead.

His men looked from the dog to the American soldier standing in the tall grass by the rice paddy with puzzlement on their faces. Then one of the soldiers shouted and pointed at Double O, and the shocked silence gave way to chaos.

The people in the doorway of the low building screamed and shoved at one another to get back inside.

The woman pulled herself from the ground and ran to her son, sweeping him up in her arms and rushing him inside to safety.

Ajax barked.

The rest of the Vietnamese soldiers scrambled out of the truck again, rushing to take up defensive positions, and they fired madly at the rice paddies. Double O threw himself back down into the water below as bullets zipped overhead like angry fireflies.

"We stepped in it, now!" yelled Billy, with that same rush of excitement he'd felt during his first battle. "We're in it, for sure!" He looked over at Double O, who was pulling himself out of the muck. "Nice shooting," he added.

"Women, children, and dogs," sighed Double O. "You mess with them, you mess with me. The warrior's code."

Billy nodded. He liked the sound of that. The warrior's code. It made their whole adventure sound more honorable, instead of crazy. "Quixotic," he said out loud, because it sounded like a word for a man who lived by a code.

Bullets sliced into the flooded field in front of them, kicking up geysers of filthy water. Chuck dared a glance over the tall grass. He saw Ajax alone in the square surrounded by soldiers whose smells he didn't know, and flinching at the loud crack of gunfire. Ajax barked, and Chuck saw the Vietnamese soldiers notice him barking. The dog had saved the boy's life, but now he was the one in danger.

Chuck stood in spite of the gunfire blazing through the brush, and he whistled. Ajax stopped barking, looked up at Chuck, and broke into a run back across the field of battle, weaving through the gunfire, racing the bullets toward his master. Chuck rushed forward to meet him, ducking the sheets of machine-gun fire tearing up the grass around him.

"Chuck, get back here!" Doc yelled, but Chuck could think only of reaching his dog, of protecting him. When they met, Ajax dove straight into Chuck, knocking him back onto the mud, as bullets slammed in all around them. Chuck grabbed the dog in a tight hug and rolled, so that he was on top, so that his body was between his dog and danger.

Ajax struggled in Chuck's arms, trying to get free. Chuck had to hold him down with both arms, his own rifle hanging uselessly over his shoulder. He started crawling back toward the cover of the rice paddy, low so that the soldiers couldn't see exactly where he was in the high grass. He dragged Ajax beneath him. The dog whimpered with fear and confusion.

"It'll be okay," Chuck comforted him. "It'll be over soon. It'll all be — *Ah!*" He felt a sharp pain in his hip, and for a moment he thought he'd been bitten by a snake. Then he felt a quick series of punches on his back that knocked the wind right out of him and he knew that he had just been shot.

He gnashed his teeth together and tried to keep moving, but he couldn't make himself go. His body wouldn't obey. Ajax panted nervously beneath him.

"You okay?" Double O called from about twenty feet away. Between the watery ditch where he and Billy and Doc were dug in, there was just open space. If he tried to make it across, the soldiers in the village square would have a clear shot at him. He was pinned down. It was a pretty good excuse not to move.

"I'm okay!" Chuck whisper-shouted back, and gave Double O a thumbs up, even though he knew it was far from the truth. He couldn't even lift his shooting arm. And the pain in his hip was extraordinary. He saw Doc looking at him nervously, but he turned his head away. He didn't want Doc to see the fear in his face.

Back in the mud, Billy asked Double O, "We going to return fire?"

"If we start shooting, they'll know our position right away," Double O said.

"They lost their commander. Without him they've got to be a little afraid," Billy answered. "If we can make them think there's more of us out here, maybe they'll run off."

"Nice thinking," said Double O. "You ain't half as dumb as you look."

"I'll slip around to the right, low in the water, and draw their fire away. Then you open up on them from this side. They'll think we've got at least two platoons out here." He pulled out one of his grenades. "I can buy us a little more cover with this."

"You do realize that the men shooting at us are allies of the United States?" said Doc.

"Sure," said Billy. "But right now I'm not fighting for the United States. I'm fighting for that boy and his mom. It's the warrior's code."

"Right on," said Double O, nodding approval at Billy. Billy smirked. He figured this would be a good story to impress Nancy Werner . . . if he survived it.

He pulled the pin from the grenade and tossed it in a high arc to their left, as far he could throw it. He didn't want it to land in the village because of all the civilians. He didn't really want to hit any of the soldiers either. He just wanted to distract them.

Seconds later, the grenade exploded with a bang, showering mud and fragments of hot metal into the air, and forcing the Vietnamese soldiers to take cover. Double O immediately popped up through the grass and fired, keeping them pinned down behind their truck and the low buildings of the village.

"Don't hit their tires," Doc called up to him. "We want them to be able to leave!"

Billy ran as fast as he could through the watery rice paddy. His heart thumped hard enough to burst out of his chest. He kept his head down and his rifle high. When he guessed he was far enough away from the others to create the illusion that there were more than four guys and a dog in the fields, he threw himself into the grass, his pants soaked and caked with mud.

He settled his gun against his shoulder and squeezed the trigger, sending a burst of gunfire into the side of the jeep in the village. One of the Vietnamese soldiers peered around and then ducked back behind the tires when Billy's bullets hit. Billy couldn't help but feel powerful.

He glanced over at Double O's position and saw the streaks of tracer fire slicing into the village. Hopefully the illusion was working. The Vietnamese soldiers were concentrated in the square while Double O and Billy fired on them from two different points. It was like a triangle of death, and Billy really hoped they'd get the point and leave.

One of the soldiers behind the personnel truck popped out and fired a few shots toward Double O. Billy shot near the man's feet, so he had to dive back behind the truck. Then he pulled out his second grenade. He hesitated. It was his last one. But he couldn't resist. He pulled the pin and chucked it overhand so that it landed near the jeep.

Right after the explosion, the prisoners streamed from the back of the truck and ran into the village to hide. The soldiers fired halfhearted shots after them. Billy squeezed off a few more rounds to keep them down, to keep them from giving chase. He saw the body of the commander lying in the mud. He saw another body, another Vietnamese soldier, lying near the crater where his grenade had hit.

He knew, right away, that he'd done that.

He'd killed a man.

He felt transfixed by the body on the ground. His eyes lingered on it. Where once there had been a man doing his job, full of life and ideas and wants — all the normal stuff of being a person — there was just a lump of uniform and flesh and bone, no life in it at all. It might as well have been a soccer ball as a person. It was just a thing.

Billy couldn't believe he'd done that. The excitement vanished, the thrill of battle gone. He did not feel the urge to smile. He felt, he realized, nothing at all. Above him the sky was gray. He wished the clouds would part so he could look up at the blue, just like in his first gunfight, so that he could remember how great it felt to be alive.

He didn't regret throwing the grenade — the man had been shooting at him, after all — but he also wasn't glad. It just seemed a waste. All this killing, and he couldn't remember why. Why was he in this village? Why was he in Vietnam at all? Shouldn't he be at the movies in Minneapolis, or slow dancing with Nancy Werner at the prom? It just made no sense to him at all.

He didn't notice that he was standing at his full height, lost in thought. He didn't notice that he'd stopped shooting. His mind was a thousand miles away.

A loud crack from a bullet whizzing by his head snapped him back to the moment, and he ducked. He returned fire, but he wasn't really looking where he was shooting. If he hit anyone else, he didn't want to know it.

Lying in the grass, not very far from Billy's position, Chuck reached around and, with his fingers, touched his back where he felt the pain blossoming like a hothouse flower. He touched the tender wound and brought his hand back around to look at his wet red fingers.

Blood. Lots of it. He'd been shot in the back, the shoulder, the leg, and the left hip. He knew right away that the mission to get Ajax to safety had just gotten a lot more complicated.

He listened to the gunfight. He could no longer see it over the grass. He couldn't stand. He heard another explosion. Double O must have thrown a grenade too. Moments later came the screech of an engine and the sound of tires squealing. The shooting had stopped; the South Vietnamese army truck was racing away.

"We won," he whispered to Ajax. "It's all okay. It's over." He felt very tired. He was relieved they'd won, and maybe now he could take a rest.

"Chuck! Chuck!" He heard his name being called, but he couldn't find his voice to answer.

He let go of Ajax, and the dog wiggled out from underneath him and ran off into the grass.

"Go get 'em," he whispered.

He waited in the grass, feeling his heart working doubly hard to pump blood through his body, even as the blood was spilling out of him. He'd been shot once before, the first time Ajax had saved him, but he knew the wound wasn't as serious that time. He stopped himself from thinking about it too much. Worry wouldn't do him any good now.

Moments later, Ajax was back, leading Double O and Billy Beans and Doc right to him. "Good boy," he said, and he looked up with a wink. "Hey, Doc."

He tried to push himself up to stand, but his leg gave out. Pain shot through his side, and he saw stars. He fell back with a splash into the mud.

"I've been shot," he explained. His tongue felt heavy in his mouth. Ajax offered the only medicine a dog knew. He licked Chuck's face.

Doc immediately bent down to examine the wounds. He ran his hands over Chuck, feeling out the gunshot in his hip and just below it in his leg, another two in the back of his shoulder, blood rushing out and muddy water soaking the wounds.

"You just stay cool, Devil Dog," said Double O. "Doc'll get you fixed up."

Chuck looked up and saw Doc's heavy face hanging over him, and he caught the worry etched on the medic's brow. Behind him, Billy shifted nervously from foot to foot.

"It isn't good, is it?" Chuck asked. His voice came out crackly. He swallowed hard and found his throat ached.

Doc took a deep breath, but didn't say anything.

"It's okay," said Chuck. "The Frenchman will help me out."

"The Frenchman," echoed Doc, and Chuck closed his eyes, just for a second, just to get some rest. He figured he'd need his strength if they were going to get to the Frenchman.

With his eyes closed, lost in his dreams, he didn't see Doc look back at Double O and at Billy and shake his head from side to side, and he didn't hear Doc whisper up to them, his voice heavy with regret, "It's not good at all."

In his dream, he was already running through an open field, Ajax barking gleefully beside him.

NEW COMPANIONS

In the village, the people shoved their meager possessions into bundles and sacks, gathering together to flee into the jungle. They feared the army would return with more soldiers to punish them and to pursue the escaped prisoners. They might burn the whole village to the ground. The villagers knew they had to leave.

Double O watched them running to and fro, gathering what food they could carry. Ajax lay at Chuck's side, his ears perked up and his senses on high alert. Whenever someone passed near Chuck, Ajax growled.

Double O watched the woman holding the boy's hand as a few of the escaped prisoners dug a small grave for her cousin. When he was in the ground, she came over to Double O.

"Thank you," she said.

Double O nodded.

"Your friend, he is hurt?" she asked.

Double O nodded again. He turned back to Doc and Billy, who were discussing what to do about Chuck. They had bandaged his wounds and stopped the bleeding as much as they could.

Ajax nudged Chuck's face with his snout, letting out small whimpers, and Billy had to pull him back to give Chuck some air. Ajax snarled at him, and Billy let him go. Chuck's breathing was shallow and his skin pale as paper.

"I don't know how long he can make it without real medical attention," said Doc. "I already lost one patient today."

The woman looked down at her feet.

On the ground, Chuck groaned.

"Hang in there, Chuck," said Double O. "You gonna be okay."

"Going to," Chuck whispered from the ground. "Right way to say it . . . *going* to be okay . . ."

Double O laughed and rubbed the back of his neck. Chuck smiled but drifted off to sleep again.

"We *have* to get him to a hospital," Doc whispered.

"What about the Frenchman?" asked Billy. He bent down to get the map out of Chuck's pocket and Ajax barked loudly at him. Billy jumped back. Ajax rested his head across Chuck's chest. "Anyway, they said it's only a day away. Maybe the Frenchman can help."

"If there is a Frenchman," said Doc.

"What do you mean, 'if'?" said Billy. "We came all this way to find him. We risked everything."

"We came all this way and risked everything because it was better than doing nothing," said Doc. "Saving that dog felt like the only thing that made sense in this crazy war. But what I know is true is that without a hospital, Chuck is going to die."

Double O sucked his teeth and looked back to the village square. The villagers had already started streaming into the jungle. No one else said a word to the Americans. No one even looked their way.

"We will lead you," the woman said. Her boy came scampering over. Ajax raised his head as the boy approached. His tail thumped on the mud.

"That's nice of you, ma'am," said Doc. "But we saw those American choppers. There have got to be more around here. It's a hot area, a lot of enemy activity." His face flushed as he realized he was talking to a woman whose cousin had been the enemy. That thought made him realize they'd just fought their allies to set a group of their enemies free. Things got so confusing in the middle of someone else's civil war.

He shook the thoughts from his head, stopped trying to untangle the mess of who was friend and who was foe. He focused on the problem in front of him, just like he'd been trained. "We can set off one of these flares we've got, pop a smoke grenade and wait for a chopper to come check it out. They'll medevac us straight back to base."

"And arrest us all as deserters," added Double O, gesturing at the shot-up village. "All this for nothing."

Ajax kept trying to nuzzle Chuck awake. He let the boy stroke the bristly brown-and-black fur on his back.

"I think Chuck would prefer jail to dying," said Doc.

"No," groaned Chuck from the ground. He could hear everything they were saying above him. "Ajax." He reached up slowly and patted the dog on the head. "We save Ajax."

The guys looked at each other, trying to communicate with their eyes. The woman nodded. "We will help you," she said.

"Listen." Chuck strained to push himself up on one arm. His voice was quiet, but clear. "I can't go back until I know

Ajax is safe," he told them. "I wouldn't have lived this long if it weren't for him. I won't give up on him now. I'll be okay."

"You've been shot in the shoulder, the leg, and the hip," said Doc. "You can't walk."

"Then leave me here," said Chuck. "Come back to get me after Ajax is okay."

"Not a chance," said Doc.

"Those soldiers will be back," the woman explained. "They know this is VC village. They will punish who they find."

"We can carry him," said Billy. "Doc and I can carry him on his poncho, like a stretcher. Double O can walk point with the woman and the boy. Ajax likes the boy. He'll listen."

The boy didn't know they were talking about him. He just petted Ajax and let the dog lick his hand.

They all thought about the idea.

"Maybe we'll make the Frenchman's place before I get worse," said Chuck. "Maybe he's got medicine or something . . ."

Doc leaned in close to Chuck. "We have no way to know if there really even is a —"

Double O put his hand on Doc's shoulder to stop him talking. "Everybody needs hope," he whispered. "All of us."

Doc bit his lip and nodded. "All right," he said. He smiled down at Chuck. "Let's go find this Frenchman and get you patched up."

Chuck nodded.

"You take the leash now," he said to the boy, straining to put the leather lead in the boy's hand. He patted Ajax, showing the boy and the dog that it was all okay. The woman explained to the boy what was happening, and his chest seemed to swell with pride at the role he got to play.

"I'm ready," said Chuck, gritting his teeth through the pain as they shifted him onto his poncho and hoisted the ends onto their shoulders. Billy took the front, and Doc took the back so he could keep his eye on Chuck.

Double O walked with the boy and his mother, and Ajax walked beside them, glancing back every few seconds to make sure his master was still behind them as he sniffed his way through the village square, now abandoned.

Chuck glanced over from his odd stretcher and noticed the boy's blue bicycle still resting against the building. There was a string of bullet holes in the wall just above it, but the bike itself was unharmed. It glistened with beads of water and kept a silent watch over the square.

Chuck could hear Ajax pulling in great gasping snorts through his snout, sealing the smells of the village in his dog brain, stored with a million other scents from the country and from the war.

Chuck wondered if Ajax remembered the pine tree smell at Fort Benning, Georgia, where they'd met, or the clean cotton scent of the nice suburban family that had raised him as a puppy before turning him over to the army. He wondered if Ajax remembered what Chuck's shampoo smelled like or if he would even remember what it was like to be clean. What smells did a dog hold on to and what smells did he forget?

Chuck wondered what would happen if they found the Frenchman and left Ajax in his care. He hadn't really thought about what they'd do next. They'd have to find the Americans and turn themselves in. He'd take full responsibility, if he could still speak by then. Maybe he could say he kidnapped the others or tricked them. It'd be a hard story to sell, what with them carrying him and still being armed.

Maybe the military court would have mercy. Maybe,

after a few years behind bars, he'd be released. He could come back to Vietnam and he could go to the Frenchman again, and Ajax would run into his arms, and he would shout, "Kiss!", and Ajax would douse him with his pink tongue, his tail wagging up a storm because he knew Chuck's smell better than any smell in the world, after all those days on patrol and nights in the foxholes and the kennel. They would fly back to the United States, first class, and Chuck would get some land out West, some place where no one would ask about his time in the war or where he got that limp, and then he and his dog could play in peace.

Chuck smiled at the thought. It was possible. Possibility was all that mattered to any of them as they walked from the village, across the fields to the misty hills.

One more day of hiking.

He would be okay, and they would find the Frenchman, and Ajax would be safe. Chuck repeated it to himself, over and over, as if thinking and thinking on what he wanted could make it so. Wanting alone was not enough, but their goal got closer with every footstep. Just on the other side of the hill, Chuck thought, anything would be possible. All it took were footsteps — footsteps in the right direction.

Chuck smiled up at the sky as his stretcher swayed like a hammock and the others slogged his weight along. He heard Ajax bark playfully.

"I'm right here, boy," he called forward in the line, letting him know. "I'm still right here."

CHAPTER 18

THE DINOSAURS IN THE JUNGLE

They hiked through the rest of the day and into the night. Ajax's nose and the woman's knowledge of the hills and paths guided them through the dark.

They stopped to rest under the cartoonishly large leaves of some sort of tropical tree. Chuck was awake, staring up. The giant trees with their giant leaves reminded him of a movie he'd seen about dinosaurs. He felt like they were in a prehistoric forest, and he began to worry about what might happen now that they had stopped.

"T-Rex," he said. "Keep quiet. Could be T-Rex out here. Giant dinosaurs."

"Shh." Doc put his hand on Chuck's good shoulder, comforting him. "You're just dreaming. We stopped to feed Ajax and take a breather."

They rummaged through Chuck's bag, and Chuck told them which were the cans of dog food and which were the cans of people food.

"Only dinosaurs out here are us," said Doc. "We're the dinosaurs."

Chuck laughed. Of course there were no dinosaurs in Vietnam. He was having trouble keeping his imagination and the real world straight. Doc put a canteen to Chuck's lips, and he drank some water, coughing and spluttering up half of it.

Right next to his ear, he heard the snort and snarl of Ajax eating his food from a ration can. He tilted his head and saw the boy still stroking the dog's broad back, awestruck.

A bolt of pain shot up his spine and sliced out through his limbs with such force that he gasped. The boy looked at him, alarmed, and his mother pulled him away. They sat off by themselves, eating something they'd brought wrapped in wide leaves, the mother whispering to her son in that way that mothers have. The words weren't really important. The tone said it all. Chuck felt better hearing it.

He could feel his heartbeat fluttering in his chest. Once the pain settled down, he shivered. The jungle night was wet and cool, but Chuck knew he wasn't cold because of the weather. He had lost a lot of blood, and that made him cold. He knew what Doc had said. He didn't want to die.

He imagined himself back home, calling Ajax over and over again, calling to his dog, but Ajax wasn't there. In his mind, he saw Griffin coming to him, holding Ajax's collar and pointing to a pit in the ground, a muddy, wet pit, and Chuck couldn't bear to look inside it.

"He's with Bruno now," said Griffin, and Chuck shuddered himself awake. His eyes snapped open. Just a nightmare.

Ajax had curled up beside him, snoring. Double O was sitting on the ground next to him, cleaning his rifle, and Billy was doing the same.

"You know, Billy," said Double O. "You did some fine fighting back there. We gonna have to change your nickname. You're no bean farmer. You cool beans, brother."

Billy smiled. "You just called me *brother*," he said.

"Well," Double O sighed. "After what we been through . . ." He let the thought fade. Chuck smirked. He felt like he'd had some role in whatever strange friendship was forming.

"What about you, Chuck?" said Billy. "We never heard from you. You ever have a nickname?"

"You keep calling me Devil Dog," said Chuck.

"I mean before that," said Double O.

Chuck shook his head. "No one ever took much notice of me," he said. "It was always about the dog. They wanted Ajax on patrols and Ajax by their foxholes . . ."

The guys glanced at one another. They'd thought the same way before.

"Ajax, though — he's got the perfect name," Chuck said. "Ajax was an ancient Greek hero — Ajax the Great. One of the strongest warriors in all the armies of Greece. And he was one of the few heroes to survive the epic Trojan War."

"That so?" Double O was impressed with what Chuck knew. He actually knew the story of Ajax himself, because his mom used to read to him from the long and ancient poem that told the story. It was called *The Iliad*, and his mother had loved it, had said it would help him to get ahead if he knew it. But Chuck was leaving off the real ending of the story of Ajax the Great. In the story, Ajax survives the war, but he never does make it home to Greece again. Maybe Chuck didn't know the ending, or maybe Chuck just didn't want to talk about it. It was only an old story, after all.

"You guys sure read a lot," said Billy.

"My mom always says a book is the best way to travel the world," said Double O.

"I think I've seen enough of the world already," said Billy.

"This ain't the world," Double O told him. "This is the war. Read a book and you'll see the world's a bigger place than all this nonsense."

"I've read books before," said Billy.

"Books without pictures?" Double O smirked at him.

Billy made a rude gesture at Double O, and much to his embarrassment, the boy sitting with his mother noticed and imitated it right away. Billy blushed.

"Good job," Doc joked. "Way to spread the finest our culture has to offer."

Chuck laughed and rubbed Ajax behind his ears. For a moment, it felt like everything was going to be okay. They were joking and talking like old times, like the good times. Then another jolt of pain shot through him. He winced. Doc rushed to his side.

"I think we should get moving again," said Chuck, his face pinched.

"All right." Doc nodded. "You guys ready?"

Double O stood and told the woman they were moving again. Billy tried to get Ajax up, but the dog snarled at him and he backed off.

"When you gonna learn?" Double O laughed. The boy came over and took the leash, and Ajax popped to his feet, eager as ever to continue. Billy shook his head.

They pushed on in the dark. Ajax sniffed curiously at the underbrush. Occasionally he pulled the boy in a wide circle around a particular patch of ground and the group followed, or he stopped to do his business on a tree, to mark his territory just like Chuck had carved their names over the ping-pong table. That felt like so long ago, back when they were undefeated.

Doc gave Chuck constant updates on what Ajax was up to, even when he wasn't sure Chuck was awake anymore. They kept moving steadily through the night.

As the sun began to rise, they felt the ground sloping down, and they knew they'd crossed the hills. Before the sun had peeked up all the way above the mountains on the horizon, the group had picked their way down into the green twilight of a river valley. They reached a swollen river and saw a rickety wooden bridge slung across it downstream.

Ajax sniffed at the river and splashed the surface with his paw. The rushing water jumped up when he smacked it, startling him back and making him sneeze. The boy giggled and splashed him. Ajax tried to bite at the spray of water, which only made him sneeze more. Watching from his makeshift stretcher, Chuck laughed.

Doc looked up, following the line of the bridge to a path on the other side of the river. He gasped. "Would you look at that!"

He could just make out a flash of white through the trees, a glimpse of marble.

"Is that — ?" Billy started.

"Looks like a mansion to me," said Double O.

Ajax barked and ran in circles around Chuck on the stretcher, yanking his leash right out of the boy's hand. Then he darted off down the river to the bridge. The boy scampered after him, taking his job as the dog handler very seriously, even as it became clear that the dog was the one in charge.

When they caught up to Ajax and the boy at the bridge, they could see the hill slope up on the other side, an overgrown path cut across it. The path turned sharply into the jungle. From here, they could just make out the angled roof of a grand house poking above the trees.

The bridge itself was made of planks of wood strung together with rope, overgrown with vines and patches of moss. It swayed in the wind over the rushing river below, and Ajax whimpered at it, planting his feet firmly.

"That bridge don't look safe to cross," said Billy.

"No, it doesn't," said Double O.

Just then, Ajax turned away from the river and looked back at the jungle. His ears pointed; the hair on his back rose, and he let out cautious growl, one front paw raised in the air.

The boy said something to his mother. She pulled him close.

"Ajax alerted," Double O said.

Chuck turned his head in the hammock with a great deal of effort and looked down at his dog, trying to read his reaction. He nearly passed out from the pain and the effort of just looking down.

"Someone's coming," Chuck said. "Not a small group, by the looks of it."

He coughed hard and winced as he coughed. When he took his hand away from his mouth, there was some blood on it. He didn't need Doc to tell him that was a bad sign, but worry would have to wait.

They had to get across the river, fast.

CHAPTER 19

ACROSS THE BRIDGE

The boy and his mother went first. They tried to pull Ajax across the bridge with them, but he wouldn't move.

"Go," said Chuck. He shooed them forward with his hand so that they would understand. The boy released the leash and they scurried to the other side. The bridge creaked, and they had to step over a spot where two planks had broken, but they made it across and crouched low in the bushes.

"Ajax will follow me across," said Chuck.

"We can't carry you," said Doc. "No way the bridge will take all that weight at the same time. No way."

"Set me down," said Chuck. "I'll walk."

"You can't walk," said Billy, although it didn't really need to be said. They all knew it was true.

"I can't *not* walk either," Chuck said. "We don't have time to argue. You guys go first, and Ajax and I will make our way after."

"I'll go last," said Billy. "That way I can cover you from this side . . . if it comes to that."

Doc shook his head. "This is a bad idea."

"It's the only idea we've got," said Double O. "And Chuck's right. No time to argue. Let's move."

With that, Double O took his first careful steps onto the swaying bridge. He paused and held tight to the ropes, whispered a short prayer to himself, and then crossed the bridge as fast as he could. When he reached the other side, he turned and knelt, lifting his rifle and aiming at the bush behind the others. He signaled for the next person to cross.

Doc nodded, and he and Billy set Chuck down carefully on the ground. Ajax immediately came to his side and sat, like a sentry on guard duty. Chuck reached over and patted him.

Doc stepped out on the bridge. He was by far the heaviest guy in the group, and sure enough, his foot went right through a plank about halfway across. He caught himself while falling, and hung for a perilous moment from the suspension rope of the bridge. But he recovered, his hand

179

burning, and he hauled himself back up and made it the rest of the way.

"Your turn," said Billy. He bent down and hoisted Chuck up under his good shoulder. He heard Chuck suck in a sharp breath, but he got him standing.

"Thanks," Chuck said, grabbing Ajax's leash in his good arm, the other one hanging limply off his bad shoulder. He leaned on his one good leg and exhaled. Billy helped him onto the first part of the bridge, leaning him on the guide rope. Ajax took a nervous step by his side. "Okay, buddy," Chuck told his dog. "I need you to save me again, so I can save you. You gotta pull me across."

Ajax looked up at him, knowing the sound of a request in his master's voice, but clearly not understanding what was expected of him. He sniffed at the planks by his feet and looked back to the bush behind them.

"Go," Chuck commanded, and that Ajax understood. He stepped forward and pulled Chuck along with him. Chuck gritted his teeth and held himself up by leaning on the side of the bridge and hopping along. The planks creaked in protest and the bridge jerked madly, but it held. "Good boy!" Chuck praised Ajax with every step, trying to sound cheerful through the agony he felt. "Good dog!"

It felt like hours before they made it across, although it could not have been more than five minutes. As soon as they reached the other side, Chuck collapsed to the ground, out of breath, tears of pain running down his cheeks. Ajax licked his face.

"You okay?" Double O was over him.

Chuck couldn't find the strength to answer. He heard Billy scampering across the bridge and felt himself being dragged into the brush. He couldn't lift his head, but he didn't dare pass out. He lay still and kept a hand resting on Ajax's side, and he listened.

Ducked under some bushes, rifles raised, Billy and Double O watched the opposite riverbank. The woman and the boy huddled behind them, and Doc lay beside Chuck, pressing his fingertips to Chuck's neck to feel his fading pulse.

"Hang in there, soldier," Doc whispered.

"Those are Americans," Billy whispered urgently. "Marines."

"Stay cool," said Double O. "Just stay cool."

Doc peered through the bushes to the other side of the river. He watched as a squad of twelve American soldiers stopped at the other end of the bridge, talking to each other and pointing across, up toward the roof of the marble house.

Double O flicked the safety catch on his gun, locking the trigger so the gun wouldn't shoot by accident. But still he held the rifle, cradled on his shoulder. It was like an extension of his arm at this point. He wouldn't feel safe setting it down, not after what had happened back in the village.

The marines stood talking for a while longer on the other side of the river. Then one of them signaled back into the bush, and two more guys came out, one of them hauling a heavy radio on his back, the antenna bobbing slightly as he walked. The other guy must be the officer in charge. He shook his head as the men talked to him and then pointed downriver. He raised his hand and pointed with two fingers and his thumb, signaling for the patrol to continue.

Double O exhaled with relief, watching the squad move on along their side. More marines slid out of the bush, following in line. They seemed to materialize from the jungle itself, covered in mud and leaves and filth, their faces worn out, the whites of their eyes flashing up as they each took turns glancing curiously toward the strange white rooftop poking out across the river.

It took ages for the platoon to pass by, but soon they were gone from sight, leaving not a clue that they had ever been there. Billy relaxed, slumping back onto his behind in the mud. He rubbed his eyes.

"How's our man?" Double O asked.

Doc felt Chuck's pulse again and shook his head. "Not good," he said. "We're losing him."

Ajax rested his snout snugly in Chuck's armpit, but Chuck didn't react. His eyes fluttered lightly behind his eyelids. His shallow breaths made a rasping noise as they came out. Ajax whimpered.

"Let's get up to the house," said Double O.

They hoisted Chuck back onto his poncho and carried him up toward the house. Ajax didn't walk in front with the boy; he stayed right underneath Chuck, walking with his head held high, sniffing urgently to keep his master's smell.

They turned the bend in the path and saw the mansion rise from the jungle in front of them, just as it had been described. Three long steps rose to a grand porch that was topped with a wide portico, supported by four high marble columns. Large windows arranged in neat rows surrounded an arched doorway. There was only one difference between the Frenchman's mansion as Billy's cousin described it in his letter and the mansion they saw before them in the jungle.

This one was a ruin.

No one lived here, and it looked as if no one had for a very long time. Moss carpeted the porch, vines crept up the marble columns, and the arched doorway gaped open, the marble floors beyond littered with leaves and dirt and tangled roots breaking through from below.

"No one's home," Double O sighed.

Billy's mouth gaped open, speechless.

"No dogs either," Double O added. "None but Ajax, anyway."

"We there?" Chuck's voice croaked out from the stretcher. He couldn't lift his head to see.

"Yeah . . ." said Doc, as comfortingly as he could. "We're here."

Staring straight up at the sky, Chuck smiled. He spoke upward, but his words were meant for Ajax, below. "I told you we'd make it, pal. I told you . . ."

Doc and Double O and Billy shared a nervous glance, wondering what to tell Chuck and what to do with Ajax. They knew that time was running out.

CHAPTER 20

THE DOG LIES

The others set Chuck down and stepped away to talk for a moment. Ajax stayed by his master's side, sniffing gently at his face. Chuck's eyes were closed, but his lips twitched with a fragment of a smile every time the big snout bumped his cheek. The dog lay snugly next to him and Chuck felt the powerful chest rising and falling with every breath, encouraging him to keep breathing too. He lay and he breathed and he let his dog lie beside him. It felt like peace.

The boy and his mother looked around the ruined mansion, peering in through the broken windows. She kept pulling the boy's curious hands away from the shards of colored glass that jutted out from the window frames. As the heat of the day settled over the hills, morning mist rose off the clearing, giving the whole scene of the ruined mansion in the jungle the look of a dream. In the distance, they heard helicopters, but the sound quickly faded away.

"We know the marines are nearby," said Doc. He pulled out his flare and a purple-smoke grenade. "I say we pop smoke. They'll come to check it out, call in one of those medevac choppers, and get Chuck the help he needs."

Double O nodded. There was no Frenchman. That really was their only choice.

"We can tell 'em we got separated from our unit," Doc said. "Marines won't know what the army's up to. By the time they sort out all the confusion, maybe we'll be safe and sound in Saigon."

"What about Ajax?" said Billy.

They turned and looked at the dog handler, lying on his poncho on the ground, his faithful dog standing guard over him, nuzzling gently to wake his master.

"If the army gets Ajax, they'll just put him down like they planned from the start," Billy said.

Ajax lay down on the poncho next to Chuck, his head resting on the ground beside his master's.

"We could just let him go," suggested Billy. "Just let him run into the jungle."

"He'll never leave Chuck's side," Double O answered.

They stood in the morning mist, thinking, trying to come up with a plan. They had to admit, they weren't much good at coming up with plans.

The ping-pong table idea hadn't worked, going into the village had been a disaster, and trying to save Ajax by taking him to a made-up Frenchman had been plain madness from the start. Quixotic, Billy decided, wasn't such a good thing at all.

"Was all this a waste?" Billy voiced his worry out loud, looking at Chuck and Ajax, but his gaze seemed to take in the ruined mansion and the jungle and the boy and his mother, the whole country even, and it was clearly a question with no answer.

"No," Double O answered anyway.

He knew it wasn't a waste. It was the only thing he'd done in the war that wasn't a waste, and he wasn't ready to give up on it now. Things didn't always have to work out for them to matter. Most things didn't work out, but Double O knew that they mattered. Life mattered, and trying to save one, even a dog's, mattered a great deal.

He looked Billy square in the eyes and told him, "I got one more plan left in me."

Billy was about to ask him what when Double O turned on his heels and jogged over to the porch to speak to the woman. As they talked, he gestured back at Chuck, explaining something to her. She nodded and held her boy close against her side, her arm wrapped around his shoulder, more affectionate than afraid.

"What could Double O be up to?" Doc wondered. "We don't have time for another ping-pong table plan . . . Those marines are going to be too far away to see us if we don't set off that flare soon."

"I think I know . . ." Billy said. "I think I get it."

Double O came trotting back over to them across the grass. "We're all set," he said. "We've got to carry Chuck back across the bridge. We'll shoot the flare and then pop the smoke grenade over there. Ajax won't follow us."

"He won't?" Doc raised an eyebrow.

"No," said Double O. "He's afraid of the bridge without Chuck holding him . . . and anyway, he's got a new family now."

He looked back at the woman and the boy, walking slowly across the grass to where Chuck and Ajax were lying. Ajax looked up as they approached. The woman hung back, and the boy stepped forward. Ajax whimpered again, but his tail wagged. The boy put his hand out, and Ajax sniffed toward it. Then he walked to the boy, licked his hand, and then stepped up to lick his face. His weight knocked the boy over, and the boy let out a surprised gasp; it sounded like a yelp.

"Play nice, Ajax," Chuck murmured, his eyes still shut. "You're not a soldier here."

Chuck still held the leash in his hand, but his grip relaxed. Ajax stepped away to play with the boy, and they rolled together on the grass, just behind Chuck's head.

"Good boy," Chuck muttered, listening to the grunts and whines of his dog at play. He didn't turn his head to look. He couldn't. But in his half-dream, he could see Ajax running through the fields around the grand mansion, playing with a pack of dogs, leaping and bounding, no worries about land mines or punji stakes or missions or foxholes. Just a dog being a dog. He smiled though his lips cracked. "Good boy," he repeated.

Double O and Billy Beans and Doc came over to him. Doc bent down to check his pulse again and to make sure he was still breathing.

"We gotta carry you back across," said Double O.

"Frenchman likes his privacy, huh?" Chuck asked.

"That's right," said Doc. "The Frenchman likes his, uh, privacy. We've got to get going."

"You want to say good-bye to Ajax?" Billy whispered.

"Nah," said Chuck. "I don't want to make it harder for him. Just let him play with the other dogs."

The guys shared a look at one another, but they didn't correct Chuck.

"He wouldn't understand good-bye." Chuck kept talking, more to himself than the others. "He knows I love him. He knows."

As they lifted him up in his poncho, his eyes fluttered open for a moment. "He having fun?" he asked.

"Yeah," said Double O, looking back at the boy playing with Ajax. He wasn't lying. The boy was laughing. Ajax had rolled onto his back in the grass, and his legs were kicking up into the air, dancing crazily at the sky, his tongue hanging out. It even looked a bit like the dog was laughing. "Ajax having fun," Double O said.

The boy's mother waved. She had made a promise. She and her son were going to save Ajax. She had sworn it, and Double O believed her.

"The dog saved my son's life," she had said.

Ajax would be okay. At least, he would be as okay as they could make him. He would be loved, which is the best anyone could hope for, and no small thing. Everyone should be so lucky.

As the soldiers made their wary way over the rickety bridge, Chuck could feel it swaying in the breeze. He could hear the river rushing below and the wood creaking under their weight, the snap of a loose plank and Doc cursing, the jolt as he steadied himself again. Chuck listened carefully for the sounds behind those sounds, for the sounds from the far bank of the river. He couldn't hear any more barking.

He had imagined the Frenchman's place would be a riot of dogs barking, like a dog pound he'd once visited with his mom when he was young, trying to convince her to let him get a dog. The plan had backfired. All the barking had only confirmed his mother's belief that dogs were loud, unruly creatures.

As they set him down on the opposite side, Chuck felt himself growing very tired. He wanted to lift his arm to wave or call out to his dog, one last good-bye, but he couldn't.

"Here goes nothing," he heard Doc say, and then he heard the hiss of a flare and the high whistle as it raced across the sky. There was a pop when it exploded, and even through closed eyes, Chuck could sense the sudden brightness above.

He heard Ajax bark on the far riverbank, a loud series of barks, sharp and high, one after the other.

Double O looked back and signaled for the woman, who knew it was time. She urged the boy to take the leash and lead Ajax away. They couldn't be there when the rest of the Americans arrived. The dog was stolen military property, after all.

Step by step, the boy pulled at Ajax, urging him, comforting him, begging him, and step by step, Ajax moved backward, away from the river. Eventually, he relaxed and trotted along with the boy toward a path that continued deeper into the hills and into the jungle. Just before they disappeared around the corner, Ajax looked back and pointed his nose in Chuck's direction across the water. His brown snout, flecked with white, worked at the air, sucking in scent. He raised his right front paw and he barked once.

The boy gave a gentle tug on the leash and Ajax turned, following, and they were gone.

Doc knelt down beside Chuck, checking his bandages, measuring his pulse over and over. There wasn't much more he could do.

"I don't hear the dogs," said Chuck, his voice just barely coming out at all.

"Oh." Doc knew he had to tell Chuck something.

"They went inside." Billy knelt down, coming to Doc's rescue. "Time to eat, you know?"

"Yeah . . ." said Chuck dreamily. "To eat."

"Uh-huh," said Doc, thinking back on the time Chuck had called him out during their ping-pong table plan. This felt so similar, but so much more serious.

"He get along with the other dogs?" Chuck's brow was beaded with sweat. The effort to speak was wearing him out.

"You should see it." Double O squatted down beside the other two, resting his hand carefully on Chuck's good shoulder. "Ajax has the run of that place. He's already top dog, you know? The others are already following him around."

Double O knew he was lying now, but sometimes a lie was the kindest thing. The truth could come later.

"Yeah." Chuck's cracked lips broke out into a smile. "That's Ajax . . ."

He couldn't find the strength to say anything more. He just lay there with his eyes closed, imagining Ajax running on the lawn of the mansion, eating his food from the Frenchman's porcelain plates and drinking from his crystal goblets, tracking muddy paw prints all over the marble floors and tearing up the fancy French furniture. He pictured Ajax curling up at night right on top of the soft mattress of a grand antique bed, lying stretched out so no other dogs could get on, and snoring loud enough through that snout of his to scare off an entire battalion.

As he lay there dreaming, he could hear the snores of his dog. The snores began to sound like the distant whine of a helicopter's engines, growing louder and louder. Chuck heard voices now, American voices, loud, weary, tough, and angry voices. He heard Doc explaining something and Double O defiant and Billy just trying to get a word in. A radio crackled, and Chuck knew he wasn't dreaming anymore. The helicopter roar became deafening, and Chuck felt himself being lifted from the ground and rushed forward, set down on the hard metal floor of a chopper.

"You're gonna be okay, soldier," someone said to him, but it was a voice he didn't know.

He strained his eyes open and glanced back, through a choppy sea of camouflage helmets and tired faces, to see Billy and Double O and Doc looking his way, worry etched across all their foreheads, and beyond them he saw just the top of the white marble mansion poking through the trees.

194

He tried to take it all in, to remember the place as much as he could. He sucked in air through his nose — a deep snort — and he tried to hold the smell, over all the engine smells and the sweat smells and the fear, to capture the memory of this place, just as Ajax would have, but his nose wasn't up to it, and he gasped for breath and felt the helicopter lurch upward.

Heavy hands held him down and stuck a needle in his arm.

He feared he would never be able to find this place again. Already, he wasn't sure if it had been a dream all along.

He tilted his head for one last look at the mansion as they rose over the treetops, but he was tilted at the wrong angle, looking up and away, out the side door and at the gray sky above instead of down at the river and the jungle and Ajax's new home.

"Good-bye, old friend," he whispered anyway, up at the sky, and he could swear over the roar of the helicopter that he heard the gleeful barks of a whole pack of dogs, running free, and Ajax barking louder than any of them.

EPILOGUE

WRITTEN IN STONE

Most of the young tourists weren't even looking up from their handheld video games or their music pods or their tiny little telephones. They didn't pay much attention to the shiny black wall in front of them, etched with thousands of names. School groups filed past as their teachers tried to keep the children's chatter to a respectful level of quiet.

"This is the Vietnam Veterans Memorial wall," a teacher told her class. "It honors members of the United States armed services who served their country and died in Vietnam between 1959 and 1975. Each name on the wall is listed by the year that service member lost his life. There are 58,272 names on the wall, including those of eight women."

"What does the cross next to some of the names mean?" a girl called out.

"Please, raise your hands," the teacher said. The girl rolled her eyes but raised her hand.

"What does the cross next to some of the names mean?" she repeated. "Some of the names have diamonds and some have crosses."

"The cross means that the soldier went missing in action during the war. No one knows for sure what happened to many of these young men. A diamond next to a name indicates that the person was killed in action."

The girl nodded and lowered her hand.

"Come along," the teacher urged. "We still have to see the Lincoln Memorial before lunch!" The class scurried on. As they went, the girl ran her fingers briefly along the black stone wall, letting the names flow beneath her fingertips like a rushing river as she followed the path with the rest of her class.

On the ground at the foot of the memorial wall, visitors had laid all sorts of items: flowers and flags, prayer cards and photos, even a pair of boots.

A gray-haired man in a flannel shirt and crisp blue jeans stood close to the wall, running his pencil back and forth over a piece of paper to make a rubbing of a name carved into the shining stone.

When he was done, he looked down at the name with the diamond beside it, exhaled, then folded the paper and put it carefully in his pocket, wincing slightly as he shifted his weight onto his bad leg. The man in the expensive suit standing beside him handed him back his cane, and he leaned on it with a feeling of relief and disappointment.

"Leg gets worse every year," Chuck said, feeling the worn rubber grip of his cane against his palm. The pain in his hip had followed him from Vietnam to the military hospital in Japan, back to the States and through his discharge from the army. It stuck with him when he started his business and when he danced with his wife at their wedding, through his children's graduations from high school and college and the birth of his grandchildren. It was with him today, standing in front of the memorial wall in Washington, DC.

"Nothing fun about getting old," said Raymond Withers, running his hand along the top of his bald head.

"You seem to be doing okay, Congressman Withers," said Chuck. "Is it against the law to call you Double O?"

"Ha!" the man Chuck knew as Double O laughed. "Since when do you care about the law?"

"Since your understanding of it got us all out of trouble back in the war," Chuck answered him.

It was true. If it hadn't been for Double O's quick thinking and even quicker reading on the law, Chuck, Billy, Doc, and Double O would have all been court-martialed and thrown in jail for running off with Ajax during the war in Vietnam. But Double O had talked their way out of it.

It helped that the army was tired of scandal and didn't want the story of what happened to all their heroic dogs running in newspapers across the country. They swept the whole thing under the rug, kept it quiet, and like so much that had happened during that war, it wasn't talked about again.

Now the two old friends watched as young men in desert camouflage stood with their fathers and grandfathers, searching out names on the memorial wall, listening to the hard-won wisdom of old soldiers, and nodding as if they understood. Maybe some of them did.

It was their generation's turn to fight the wars that the generations before them no longer could. Double O watched them with sadness and with pride. He'd been so angry at the government back when he was their age, and now here he was, over forty years later, and he *was* the government, an elected congressman. Who would have thought?

"Billy's late," said Chuck, looking at his watch and then looking up at the wall. All the names. Some of them he'd known. Most of them he hadn't.

"Here he comes now," said Double O, pointing behind him.

Chuck turned and saw Billy strolling down the path along the wall, his short beard neatly trimmed, his hair thick and dark, not a speck of gray in it. He waved happily as he approached.

"The famous author arrives at last," Double O called out, hugging Billy the moment he reached them. Chuck did the same. "I read your latest novel," Double O announced, "and I think the critics got it all wrong."

"But the critics loved it," Billy answered him.

"Oh, I know," said Double O.

Billy frowned, and then Double O broke out into a big smile and let out a deep belly laugh.

"Forty years later, and you two are still driving each other crazy," sighed Chuck.

"What else are friends for?" said Double O.

"Well, I thought it was a beautiful book," said Chuck. "Even if you got most of the facts wrong."

"It's a story," said Billy. "The facts don't all need to be right for the story to be true. Sometimes, it's the facts that get in the way of truth."

"Deep thoughts, Billy. Real deep," said Double O.

They all turned to consider what Billy had said and to look at the wall in silent thought for a moment. Chuck pulled the folded paper from his pocket and handed it to Billy, who unfolded it and read the pencil rubbing of the name: Robert Malloy.

"They should have put *Doc* on there," said Billy.

"You know how many *Doc*s there were in the US Army?" said Double O. "The wall would have to be twice as large to make all those nicknames fit."

"Maybe it *should* be twice as large," said Billy. He studied his own reflection in it, looking through the thousands of names at himself in the blazer and khaki pants that Nancy had packed for him. He would have just shoved them into his suitcase like he used to pack a duffel bag, but Nancy folded them neatly. She said she wouldn't let him travel all this way to look a mess when he saw the congressman, even if they were old war buddies.

"I never could understand why Doc chose to stay in combat after everything we went through." Billy sighed.

"Guess he still thought he could save some lives," said Chuck. "After he saved mine."

They got quiet again, each of them remembering that day by the river so many years ago.

"You know I broke my promise," Chuck said. "I told Ajax I'd never leave him. But I did leave him."

"You didn't have much choice," said Billy.

Looking at all the names on the wall in front of him, Chuck remembered carving his name into the tree by the ping-pong table. "Chuck P + Ajax were here. Devil Dogs. Undefeated," he'd written.

But he guessed they *were* defeated. The war had defeated them in the end. "Ajax's name should be on that wall," he declared. "And Bruno's. And all those dogs who never came home. There should be a memorial for the canine heroes who gave their lives."

"Maybe so," said Billy. "Maybe so. But Ajax wouldn't be on it."

"What?" said Chuck.

"The wall's for heroes who were lost in the war, right?" said Billy.

"Right," said Chuck.

"Well, Ajax wasn't lost," said Billy. He looked at Double O and gave him a wink. "Tell him."

Double O nodded and smirked at Chuck. "I just got back from a congressional delegation to Vietnam last week," he said. "That's why I called you to meet here today."

"Still as charming a country as ever?" Chuck said sarcastically.

"Quite," said Double O without any sarcasm at all. "While I was over there, I had some folks do some poking around for me, asking some questions. And, well . . ."

He pulled out his digital camera and showed Chuck a picture on the screen. It was a picture of a middle-aged Vietnamese man in a white lab coat, standing behind a desk. The nameplate on the desk read *Dr. Nguyễn Chi, Veterinarian.*

"Best small-animal veterinarian in Vietnam," said Double O.

"Why are you telling me about him?" Chuck wondered.

"Well, I went to see him," said Double O. "And we talked for a long time. He told me how he got his start caring for animals. It was during the war. It was a dog he had . . . a dog some Americans left with him and his mom."

"No way," said Chuck. He pictured the boy from that village, clear as day. The boy riding his bike. The boy playing with Ajax. The gunfire.

Double O nodded. He reached into his pocket and pulled out an old photograph and handed it to Chuck.

"He wanted you to have that," he said.

Chuck took the black-and-white photo and studied it. There was a Vietnamese teenager sitting on the ground outside of a bamboo hut, smiling widely at the camera with his arms wrapped around a panting German shepherd sitting next to him. The dog sat proudly, his chest broad and healthy. His coat shined, and his eyes gleamed brightly. His ears were pointed high to the heavens and he was, to Chuck, unmistakable.

"Ajax," he said aloud.

"Dr. Chi told me that Ajax fled with him and his mother across the border into Laos. He helped them avoid soldiers and booby traps, and he kept bandits away."

"That's Ajax all right," said Chuck.

"That picture right there is from four years after we left," said Double O. "The doctor says that for the rest of his life, Ajax wagged his tail whenever he saw an American, but as soon as they got close enough to recognize, he stopped . . ."

"He was waiting for me to come back," sniffled Chuck, wiping his eyes.

"Dr. Chi says Ajax lived another three years after that picture was taken," said Double O. "And sired more than one litter of puppies." He pulled out another photo, this one in color, of tiny, little German shepherd puppies assembled in the boy's lap.

"Little Ajaxes running around Vietnam, huh?" said Chuck, laughing and letting the tears run down his cheeks.

"That's right," said Billy.

"The doctor told me that when Ajax got old and gray in the snout, he was still just the sweetest old dog, as playful as ever, if a bit slower." Double O put his hand on Chuck's shoulder. "He had a bad hip at the end."

Chuck looked down at his own cane.

Double O nodded. "He said Ajax passed away peacefully one afternoon, lying in the shade of a rubber tree."

"Ajax loved lying in the shade of those rubber trees," said Chuck.

Double O nodded. "He did, indeed."

Billy rested his hand on Chuck's shoulder too, and the three of them stood side by side in front of the wall, looking at the list of names, filled with friends and filled with strangers, and looking through the names at their own reflections and at the reflection of the Washington Monument behind them, pointing into the sky.

Children flowed around them, most not even looking up from their little electronic gadgets, but one or two did look up, perhaps wondering about these three old men, each so different, wondering how they knew one another, and why they were crying, and maybe wondering what stories they had to tell.

Chuck thought about their stories too, about ping-pong and booby traps, about their journey through the jungle to save his dog. They had to have been crazy to do something so dangerous, so reckless.

No, not crazy, he thought.

Quixotic was the word they'd used.

As he leaned on his cane and felt his friends' hands on his shoulders, he imagined Ajax again, snoozing under his rubber tree, pointy ears twitching at the sky, and he smiled.

If Chuck had to do it all again, he knew for a fact that he would.

The war in Vietnam was one of the most controversial armed conflicts in which the United States was involved during the twentieth century. It was fought mostly from 1957 to 1973 in Southeast Asia, with the Americans fighting on the side of the South Vietnamese against the communist-ruled North Vietnamese. At its height, there were over half a million American soldiers in Vietnam.

While many of the fighting men had volunteered to serve in the armed forces, many more were drafted into military service through a lottery, which was said to take an unfair number of lower income and minority young men and send them into the most dangerous jobs. In 1969, one of the most intense years of fighting for American forces, nearly 90 percent of the infantry riflemen were draftees. The war became very unpopular in the United States, and protests shook the country. Soldiers returning from war were often met with scorn rather than gratitude as the public grew disgusted with the violence in Vietnam.

A lot has been written about that time in America, but not much has been written about the dogs that served alongside the men. In large part, these dogs were donated to the military by civilians and then trained and partnered with a handler overseas. The handlers and their dogs rotated among units, going where they were needed and only staying for a little while. The handlers developed a community with one another, but mostly, they bonded with their dogs, performing some of the most dangerous tasks in the war, from walking point on patrols to clearing tunnels to searching for land mines. Over four thousand dogs served during the war in Vietnam, and sadly, none were able to return home.

A fear of tropical diseases and widespread infection among the military dogs demanded that some brave canine soldiers had to be put down to ease their suffering, while many more were simply deemed "surplus equipment" and either turned over to the South Vietnamese army or put to sleep. It was a terrible way to thank the dogs for their service and devastating for the handlers and the veterinarians involved. Countless dogs simply went missing during the conflict, and some were said to have been smuggled out.

This is a work of fiction, but it is also a kind of memorial for those lost dogs, my own quixotic dream of how some might have survived through the bravery, courage, and kindness of Americans and Vietnamese alike. It is possible. War often brings out the worst in people, but it can also bring out the best.

I would like to thank some of the heroes who helped me tell this story: Retired General John Galvin, Retired LTG Pete Taylor, and Dr. Gary Gosney, especially, who set me right on a lot of things about the care of scout dogs in Vietnam. I took their wisdom to heart, although sometimes fact had to surrender to story. All the errors and omissions in this book are purely my own.

Additionally, *A Soldier's Best Friend: Scout Dogs and Their Handlers in the Vietnam War* by John C. Burnam, who served as a scout-dog handler in Vietnam and now advocates for the National War Dogs Monument, and *None Came Home: The War Dogs of Vietnam* by Sgt. John E. O'Donnell provided valuable information and insight into the life and work of Vietnam War scout dogs and the humans who served with them.

I owe a debt to the astounding and brave writing in Karl Marlantes' tale of a few marines during the Vietnam War, *Matterhorn: A Novel of the Vietnam War* (which is where I got that gross leech story that Billy tells), and have, in small ways and large, drawn the inspiration for this tale from Tim O'Brien's 1978 novel of the Vietnam War, *Going After Cacciato*. My first paragraph is based on its first paragraph, which is my way of saying thank you. Without O'Brien's profound story, I never would have realized how to save Ajax. What wasn't possible in history is made possible by dreamers.